CELLAR DOORS

A Novel

Lance LaCoax

Cellar Doors

Visit **www.cellardoorsbook.com**

Published by Morehouse Media Group, Inc.
Franklin, Tennessee
www.morehousemediagroup.com

MOREHOUSE
MEDIA GROUP

ISBN 978-0-61546-497-8

Cover Design by Shawn Ide
Cross Cover Image Copyright Morphart, 2011
Used under license from Shutterstock.com

Printed in the United States of America

In memory of Ewe, Mom

Lance LaCoax

CELLAR DOORS

A Novel

MOREHOUSE
MEDIA GROUP

Prologue

Next Friday

Another winter storm blots the dusk sky with swirling shades of grey. Just off Highway 110, a farmhouse leans against the February freeze, settling in for a long night. Bare limbs sway in the shifting moonlight, projecting slithering shadows through vacant windows. Surrounding the house, gusts of wind comb the field of winter rye like frigid fingers through coarse hair.

At a glance, the house looks tranquil.

Sleeping.

But if you wait and listen, you can sense the unrest; a slight wheezing in the rafters as the attic breathes dusty air through its wooden ribcage. Kitchen cabinet doors squeak and shift on worn hinges and windowpanes whistle softly with each tug of wind.

The smell of burning wood hangs in the living room, though the fireplace has been cold for hours. Framed snapshots of a smiling, blonde-haired girl decorate an oak mantel. And at the base of the hearth, a Bible verse in needlepoint lies shredded and tangled in broken glass.

Most of the curtains and framed pictures have been pulled down in an obvious hurry, and throughout each room, cardboard boxes squat in varied stages of being packed.

Night air pours through the shattered window of a back bedroom. A little girl's room. The draft snakes through the house, rustling through boxes of clothes and toys. Dried blood on her lavender curtains whisper a violent story.

Something has happened here.

Something is still happening here.

Unseen fingers scratch and pry at her bedroom door, trying to get in. And in the darkness, just below the groan of the wind, a soft clicking, like the nails of a dog, roam the hardwood hallway.

Even though there is no one home, the house is not empty.

1

Last Friday

"**B**rown. I'm having a brown-colored day."

"That's not what I meant, Tim, and you know it. Think in terms of emotions. Are you happy? Then you're having a yellow day. Depressed, then it's a black day. Use the color chart to express your emotional wellness."

"I know what you mean, Doc. And my name's still Ted."

Ted hated his therapist for a multitude of reasons. He knew he'd never live in a house as nice as hers, never draw the same paycheck, or hobnob with her caliber of society. *Or drink her expensive bottled water*, he thought, glancing at the sparkling lime-flavored Perrier glistening proudly on her desk.

But mostly, he hated her arrogance. The way she looked down her horn-rimmed glasses at him. She made him feel so small.

"Let's discuss your drinking problem," she said, changing gears.

"I don't *have* a drinking problem," Ted grumbled, rolling the words *drinking problem* around his mouth distastefully.

She responded by scribbling something in her notebook and offering him that lofty smile. Ted glanced at his white knuckles gripping the armchair; his imagination flirting with ways to wipe that pompous smirk off her face. His first inclination was to jump across the desk and madly club her in the head with her fancy bottled water.

"Now who's got the drinking problem!?" He would point and laugh hysterically. But he didn't. Instead, he dismissed the fantasy and cleared his throat. "I'm a social drinker. I just don't happen to have a social life."

She scribbled again.

Ted squeezed his eyes shut preparing for the onslaught of whatever grand, self-helping revelation she was about to dump on him. His recently wrecked life had resulted in a string of DUI's and an altercation with a bagboy at Kroger. *If only he would've double-bagged...*

"Ted, are you listening to my instructions? I need you to keep a journal. Make notes of your daily regimen. It's very important to your healing process."

"Right, Doc." He opened his eyes. "You want me to keep a diary. That'll work wonders for my self-esteem."

2

Ink & Baud Building

In the industrial park forty minutes west of Willow, the second floor of the *Ink & Baud Building* held a wood-paneled boardroom with a mahogany table and a half-dozen matching chairs. Today, four of those chairs were occupied. At the head of the table, a man in a charcoal suit flipped through a folder before speaking in soft monotone.

"We are on track with the shipment going west?" He looked up from the folder expecting a confirmation from someone.

"Yes," a feminine voice responded. "We are on schedule as promised. Payment cleared yesterday, and five additional units have already been requested for the Vernal Equinox next month."

"Good," the man said, turning a page in his folder. "What about the woman; has she been located? And what of my property?"

"Nothing yet," a man sitting to his left spoke up, "but I'm optimistic we're close to a resolution."

"I'm not interested in your optimism." The man's eyes flashed. "Do I need to remind you of the serious nature of this situation? Your inability to rectify this is fast becoming a problem in itself."

The man cleared his throat; his response was less than sure. "I understand. They will be found."

Cellar Doors

3

The streets were deserted as Ted maneuvered down the block to the second stop sign, turning left toward the Shell station. He rubbed his hands together as the defroster rattled loudly, trying to generate warmth against the February night. Streetlights flashed across the hood of his car, up the windshield and over the top, causing a strobe light effect in the backseat.

He topped a small hill, and the vacant gas station came into view. Piercing red letters bathed the parking lot in a crimson light.

Something in the backseat caught his eye.

He leaned forward, searching his rear-view mirror. Something moved back there. *Was someone lying on the floorboard?* He craned his neck, waiting for the next streetlight to pass over. A twinkle, like silver eyes, flashed from the floorboard. A rush of adrenaline caused him to jerk the wheel, throwing gravel from the shoulder under his car. The light washed over the backseat, exposing nothing but a discarded burger wrapper and some junk he found at a yard sale. He took a deep breath and let the air out through his teeth. But something still didn't feel right.

Ahead, he didn't notice the 'S' on the Shell sign dim and flicker twice before shorting out completely.

He wheeled past the gas pumps into a handicap parking spot. A cheerful jingle met him as he pushed into a smog of greasy chicken and cigarette smoke.

"Got any aspirin?" Ted fumbled through the mixed nuts section before approaching the register. "I just left my therapist. Her whiny voice is still ringing in my ears."

The attendant leaned on the counter. "Looks like all we have are gel-caps," he smiled with dark eyes.

"They'll do," Ted tossed the peanuts on the counter and dug for his wallet. As an afterthought, he glanced over the attendant's shoulder at his car. The uneasy feeling was still there.

"Don't worry about it," the attendant pushed the money back to Ted. "It's in the house tonight."

"In the house?" Ted glanced at the man.

The man's crooked smile lingered. "On the house. My mistake."

The drive back to the trailer park was fast and reckless as Ted perched on the edge of his seat, afraid to lean back. Nervous sweat dripped from the end of his nose.

"This is ridiculous!" he stammered under his breath, trying to shame the nagging fear that had settled across his shoulders like a snake. Something about the gas station clerk had him creeped out. Or maybe it was just the lingering effects of his therapy session. Fortunately, no one was around to see him blaze through both stop signs and race down the dead-end street to his trailer.

Stumbling through the kitchen to his bedroom, he kicked off his shoes and dropped his jacket on the floor.

From the safety of his bedroom, he peered back down the hallway. Rubbing the back of his neck, he attempted to mash down sprouting goose bumps. *If my therapist ever finds out about this...*He slid under the sheet and reached to click off the bedside lamp.

Hesitated.

Decided to leave it on awhile. Despite sweat trickling down his neck, he pulled the covers over his head and squeezed his eyes shut.

He realized he'd left his gel caps and peanuts in the car, but had no intention of going back for them now.

Outside, a rush of wind tossed a garbage can, scattering trash across the yard.

Ted's Toyota sat at an odd angle in the driveway, a faint aura of heat dissipating from the hood. The motor clicked gently, cooling down. Suddenly, the rear of the car shifted as if weight had been loaded onto the suspension. The shocks squeaked in protest, shuddering under the load.

Across the street, a dog growled softly.

Cellar Doors

4

K at closed the door to her bedroom and carefully locked the latch. She didn't want her grandmother to know she was still awake. The wooden floor slats creaked as she moved across the room to her bed.

3:30 in the morning; another sleepless night.

She paused at the window and peered into the darkness. Silent flakes of snow drifted and swirled around the windowsill. She watched them cascade and gather.

Any other time, the delicate snow against a starless night may have inspired her to write something poetic. But tonight wasn't a night for poetry. Tonight, her thoughts were in a dark place. She glanced at the mirror over her bureau. Her straight, black hair shadowed jade eyes. A lone strand of pink hair curled around her ear. She looked away, ashamed. The little voices swirled like snow in her head.

She had done terrible things.

Unspeakable things.

The voices took sadistic pleasure in reminding her of her secrets. Dark secrets. How had she gotten into this? How did she let it get this far? She met the eyes in the mirror again but didn't recognize the person staring back at her. Not anymore.

A bellow of wind gently rattled the window, piling the snow into little pointed drifts against the pane. Jagged points of snow that resembled teeth.

Her hands began to shake as the voices whispered to her, taunting her. She tightened her hands into fists, pulling the skin taut around her knuckles. Scrawled down her left wrist, the word 'Black' was inked in blocky calligraphy. Down her right wrist was the name 'Kat.' She remembered the tattoo artist smiling when she told him her name. "Katrina," she said, chewing her bottom lip. "But everyone calls me Kat." She remembered his eyes, cobalt blue. And he had dimples; she liked dimples.

She was happy then. Sixteen, with the whole world in front of her. So much of life yet to be lived; so many dreams still waiting to come true.

But now, that life was over. She stared at her wrists and her smile vanished. Now the nickname mocked her. A constant, sick reminder of what she had become. She turned her attention to the music box on top of her bureau. The small red box had been a gift from her father.

Her dead father.

She snapped the lid open, but there was no happy, whimsical greeting. No spinning ballerina. She vaguely remembered pulling out the tinkling mechanism in a hateful rage. It didn't matter now anyway; there was no room in her life for joy—whether it was the contrived, mechanical sort, or real heartfelt happiness. Those emotions had abandoned her long ago; stripped away along with her parents, her little brother and her happy life. Her existence had been nothing more than a dark spiral since the accident; a black hole in her soul that didn't allow for the bright things of life to seep in.

No, she didn't deserve happiness. She didn't deserve mercy or joy, or any of those warm, fuzzy emotions.

Her mood grew dark as she dropped her hand into the box. It came out with a pen-shaped hobby knife with a pearl handle. Tinges of adrenaline spidered down her spine as she popped the plastic cap from the blade. She leaned against her mattress, pausing to watch the snowfall. The swirling voices had become quiet. Waiting. Only the steady throb of her heart was in her ears.

The knife was cool against her forearm. It bit deep. Tingling. A crimson pool snaked around the blade and ran toward her elbow. She worked methodically, raising and dropping the blade; following a pattern in her mind. Moments later, the knife dropped to the floor. Kat's attention was drawn back to the snowscape outside her window. For a brief moment, she felt...relief. A fleeting sense of clarity followed by a tired ache. The euphoric high faded and succumbed to the familiar heaviness of guilt and despair. Her eyes drifted down to the jagged words etched on her forearm just above 'Kat.'

HATE ME.

And she did.
It was almost poetic.

Cellar Doors

5

Ted sat up, eyes wide open. The bedroom was dark and humid. At the foot of the bed, he could barely distinguish the outline of someone standing. The silhouette was motionless and tall; crowding the ceiling. He was about to say something, but his breath caught in his throat. A building pressure in his chest squeezed and kneaded his lungs like invisible hands holding him down.

His panicked heart slammed against his ribcage, beating arrhythmically. He tried to reach for the bedside lamp, but his arm was so heavy. The room became darker. Stifling. And the air grew thick and oppressive. His eyes watered as he watched the form at the foot of the bed jerk awkwardly to the left, expand, and move closer.

Wrapped in his sweat-soaked sheet, he gulped a mouthful of air as his heart stuttered. The form weaved across the sheet toward his face. With one last surge of determination, he screamed long and loud before a tight, burning sensation stifled his cry. His lungs stung as he choked for air. His chest constricted as his stomach convulsed, expelling a mouthful of bile.

A dull crunch followed the popping of bones, and a wet gurgle issued from his chest. He watched the darkness detach and slide slowly into the shadows.

And then, there was nothing but the sensation of falling.

Across the street, the dog backed into the shadows, whimpering in the darkness.

Cellar Doors

6

"*At age 5, my little sister was eaten by wolves. She strayed deep into the woods while the family slept. Mother took it the hardest; Father never spoke of it. And I was never able to sleep alone after that night...*"

Jude folded the top corner of the manuscript's page and tossed it on the couch. "Where do they come up with this nonsense?" He couldn't help but smile.

The aroma of brewed chicory filled the kitchen as he selected a clean cup from the dishwasher, and settled on a barstool overlooking the dead grass in the backyard. Sipping the coffee, he replayed the conversation with Gwen from the night before. An art gallery in San Diego offered her a position as a buyer. She needed to make a decision soon. Jude watched a squirrel forage for scattered seed around the birdfeeder. He wasn't sure how to feel; he'd only known her a few months, but was finding it difficult to imagine life without her. And a new job in California was so far away.

He drained the cup, grabbed his jacket, and headed out the back door for the farmer's market. He had been planning a special dinner for a couple days now. But in light of Gwen's offer, he was wondering if it would be their last meal as a couple.

Jude circled the town square searching for a parking spot. The farmer's market was one of the few places in Willow that promised local, organic produce. Parking his Chevy, Jude weaved around bushels and boxes, singling out old man Leander's booth. Even in the dead of winter, Leander somehow managed to offer an array of produce that rivaled even the bigger grocery store chains.

"How's it goin', Leander?" Jude found him leaned against his truck sorting green tomatoes.

"Hey, buddy." Leander smiled. "I'm still alive, how'r you?"

"I need some strawberries. And maybe a few red potatoes."

"Sure, I got those."

"Putting together a going away dinner for my girlfriend." Jude offered.

"No kidding. Where's she off to?"

"Job opportunity in California. It's really great news for her."

"Great news for her, you say." Leander heaved a basket of potatoes off the bed of his truck. "And what about for you?"

Jude dropped his eyes. "I'll be fine. I just don't want to get in her way. You know, influence her decision. I don't think it would be fair to come between her and her dream job."

"Really?" Leander squinted at Jude. "You're breaking up over a job?" He shook some of the potatoes into a bag and held it out for Jude to take.

"Well, not breaking up; just giving her space," Jude said. "I've put a lot of thought into this. She should decide what's best for her without worrying what I think. You know, kind of like the song says, *If you love someone, set them free.*"

Leander smiled. "You really care about this girl?"

"Absolutely."

"You know, that whole caged-bird philosophy sounds romantic in poetry and song lyrics, but I think deep down, people just need to feel wanted. Maybe she needs to know she's worth pursuing." Leander handed Jude his change. "I don't know your girlfriend, but I know people. You might be making a mistake."

Jude took the change. "Trust me, I know Gwen."

7

The tow truck pulled up to a rusty singlewide at the end of a cul-de-sac in the Morning Star Mobile Home Park. The brake lights flashed as the motor shifted into park. Two men slid from the cab and paused in front of the driveway.

"This it?" A tall man with dark, shoulder-length hair adjusted his stocking cap and walked to the Toyota parked sideways in the driveway.

"1305 East 13th. Number's spray-painted on the front door, which is hanging wide open, I might add. Very classy, wouldn't you say?" The second man pulled his hoodie over his shaved head and glanced around the trailer park. "What a way to end the week." He flipped a stubby cigarette to the pavement and turned his attention to the repossession order in his hand.

"'97 green Toyota Corolla belonging to a Ted Childs; I'm sure this is it, but I'll check the VIN to be sure." The bald man glanced at the front door again. "I don't want to be around when this guy realizes what we're doing. It would be a real drag to be shot by a crack-head on the last day of the work-week."

"Josh, living in a trailer park doesn't make you a crack-head."

Peering through the windshield, Josh nodded. "Whatever, Eric. Okay, this is it. Back in and winch it up."

Eric pulled the truck around and cornered the Toyota. Within minutes, they ratcheted and secured the car and were pulling out of the drive.

"I feel a little sorry for him," Eric confessed, watching the trailer grow smaller in his side mirror. "I mean, what if he's got kids?"

"Yep, it's a real hard-knock life," Josh lit another cigarette. "Besides, that's why they invented public transportation, right?" He drummed the dash and stomped the floorboard. *"If you don't pay the bills, the repo man'll take your wheels,"* he sang his made-up chorus a couple times before losing interest and pulling a deep drag from his cigarette.

"I don't know. Sometimes I think you enjoy this job a little too much." Eric blinked irritably at the cigarette smoke. "Personally, I'm beginning to hate it about as much as your singing and your chain smoking."

"Relax, man. You got it all wrong. The way I see it, we're doing this guy a favor." He blew a smoke ring and watched it roll toward the cracked window. "Look at the junky car we're towing. I mean, now he'll be forced to get something with a little more sophistication...a nice German sedan or a Mustang maybe."

"Right. I'm sure he just lives in this trailer park for the schools."

At the impound yard, they unhitched the Corolla and cranked the lift chains back onto the truck bed.

"I'll check inside the car. Be sure he didn't leave any kids or kittens in there." Josh smiled and inhaled the last drag from his cigarette.

"Come on, buddy, you know the rules. Just leave it, and let's go home." Eric pulled the keys from the tow truck's ignition and walked toward the office.

Josh smirked at his retreating co-worker and pulled the passenger's side door open. He rifled through the glove box, then the backseat, emerging with an armful of stuff. "Hey, wait up! Don't you need a blender? What about a Van Halen shirt?"

Josh patted down a stained pair of blue jeans and found a silver necklace curled in the front pocket. He jogged behind Eric and shoved the lidless appliance at him.

"Cut it out, Josh. The guy's got enough problems without you ripping off his blender."

"Right, like he's going to miss a busted blender." Josh laughed, dropping the blender and following Eric to the office.

Inside, Eric punched his time card, waved good-bye to a sour-faced woman behind a desk, and ducked into the restroom to wash his hands. Josh pushed open the door behind him.

"You coming over tonight? Figured we grab some Chinese and a movie," Josh asked.

"You need a girlfriend. Besides, I need to drop by the station. My aunt'll need some help." Eric pulled his stocking cap off his head; his dark hair fell below his ears.

"Not to mention your apartment is a dump." Eric smiled. "Last time I was there, we couldn't even find the TV."

"That's an exaggeration, and you know it." Josh pulled the Van Halen tee over his head. "It was hiding under that mountain of laundry the whole time."

"You do realize you're a hoarder," Eric said. "Just like on TV. Pretty sure you need psychological attention."

Josh raked his fingers through his goatee, resting them on the stolen silver pendant hanging from his neck. "If I had a bigger place, it would all fit. So, are you coming over or what?"

"I don't know. Maybe."

"Well, when you finish pumping gas, drop by. And bring beer."

Cellar Doors

8

Josh Malone had never been mistaken for the philosophical or intellectual type. Standing just shy of six feet, his height pretty well summed up his life: almost there, but not quite. He sported the shaved-head and long goatee look, which he felt gave him that dangerous gangsta vibe. But most would agree his lack of hair and skinny frame only accentuated his oversized ears.

Swinging into the parking lot of the Movie Mania, he pulled open the glass doors and smiled at the sales clerk as he made a line for the new release movies on the far wall.

"What's new that's good?" He yelled over his shoulder.

The girl continued to attach bar code stickers to a stack of movies without looking up.

Josh snorted and flipped over a Blu-ray case to check the rating.

"PG-13, probably not enough blood." He pushed it back on the shelf and scanned a few more titles before deciding on something with gratuitous gore and minimal plot.

"I need your membership card." The girl looked up from her chore, a little annoyed with the distraction of having to deal with a customer.

Josh slapped his front pockets as if expecting the card to magically appear. "Must have left it at home. But it's okay, I'm a regular."

She stared at him.

"Really, I come in here all the time…Kat." He squinted at her nametag.

Kat let out an audible sigh and asked for his phone number. A strand of pink separated from her otherwise goth-black hair and fell in front of her face. She rattled her fingers across the computer's keyboard.

"Josh Malone?"

"That's me," he replied, stroking the pendant hanging from his neck.

"You've got a sixteen dollar late fee. You can pay half now, and half next time if you want."

"Sixteen dollars!" Josh feigned surprise. "I don't have sixteen dollars. Baby, don't make me go find a RedBox." His attempt at wit was punctuated with a quick wink.

"Look, I don't have time for this. Do you want the movie or not?" Kat replied coolly, tucking the defiant pink strand behind her ear.

"Uh, yeah. I'm just kidding." The sting of rejection warmed the tips of his ears beet red. He opened his wallet and took out a solitary bill. "So much for Chinese," he mumbled, offering her the money.

"Nice pendant, by the way." Her tone was noticeably softer.

"Oh, sure. Thanks," Josh felt his bruised ego beginning to recuperate. "So, maybe I'll let you wear it sometime."

Kat glanced at the pendant and then his oversized ears. "Not a chance," she said, shifting her attention back to the stack of movies.

9

1305 East 13th Morning Star Trailer Park

Sheriff Roy Rodgers heaved himself from the squad car with a painful grunt. He paused, testing the loyalty of his sore hip while smoothing down a patch of wrinkles that harassed his sports coat. The jacket had been a gift from his wife the year before she passed away. Ten years and forty pounds later, he still wore it in her memory.

On his way to the porch, the sheriff passed the man who had evidently called 911. He smelled like vomit, and his hands were shaking as he gestured to the deputy taking his statement.

There was no car in the driveway, and Saturday's mail was still in the box. *The devil's always in the details.*

"Get the MagLite, JD," he called to a lanky deputy behind him as he approached the front door.

They entered the house which was still warm even though the front door was cracked open. Leaves were scattered around the living room floor, and the smell of death hung like a curtain.

"Well, we know he didn't freeze to death," JD said, pecking the wall thermostat.

Sheriff Roy stopped at the phone. No messages. A handful of unopened bills lay scattered on the kitchen counter. JD disappeared toward the back of the house.

"Back here, Sheriff." his voice rang with hurried excitement.

Sheriff Roy joined his deputy in the back bedroom. The body was in the middle of the bed, waxy eyes fixed on the ceiling. His fingers were curled into claws, his pale lips parted.

"I'd say he's been dead awhile," JD reported as the sheriff flipped to a fresh page in his notebook. "No signs of struggle. Nothing looks to be missing. Natural causes—probably a heart attack." JD glanced at the sheriff as if expecting some congratulatory recognition for his quick deduction. Sheriff Roy picked up a journal from the floor, ignoring the deputy.

"Call the coroner, JD."

10

Josh slowed to roll over the speed bump in front of his apartment complex. He flipped a spent cigarette out the window and pulled his Nova into an empty slot in front of Building C. Clutching his movie in one hand, he juggled a warm bag of chicken fingers in the other. Thankfully, the Chunky Chicken still had the 'One Buck' menu.

He skipped up a flight of stairs to the second level and pushed open the door to his apartment. Kicking a month's mound of laundry out of the way, he dropped his dinner and movie next to the television, pulled off his shirt, and kicked his jeans to the floor. Wearing nothing but his newly stolen ram's horn necklace, he negotiated his way through the clutter to the shower.

The water was so hot it stung his skin. Josh lathered his hands and scrubbed his face and head. With a face full of soap, he reached for the loofah sponge nestled in the bath buddy hanging just under the showerhead. Just as his fingers located the sponge, something prickly brushed against his forearm.

"Whoa!" Josh exclaimed, stepping backward and forcing his eyes open. The soap burned, causing him to squint and drop the sponge. Feeling his feet slip beneath him, he grabbed blindly, clutching the plastic shower curtain. As his feet jerked forward, the plastic curtain clips popped in succession, dropping him in a flailing heap on the bathroom floor. He screamed in pain and dug at his eyes, kicking at the shower curtain that had tangled around his ankles. The room spun and tilted. Josh felt his ears pop, like the air pressure in the room had changed. He screamed again, but the sound was garbled, like his head was under water. He folded his knees and jerked his head up, only to catch the bottom of the porcelain sink with the back of his skull. A flash of lightning coursed through his mind, and the salty taste of blood filled his mouth. He fell forward limply, rolling to his side, eyes wide open in spite of the pain.

In the doorway, a dark fog began to expand, taking a human shape. It was tall, crowding the nine-foot ceiling. Josh heard a guttural noise coming from the mist as it moved closer, eclipsing the fluorescent light above the sink.

In a swift motion, the darkness consumed Josh. Ripping. Biting. Tearing at his flesh. Josh swung his arms wildly, cursing the thing that tore at him. It attacked him relentlessly, puncturing his skin and muscle, exposing sinews and bone.

Then, as quickly as it had come, it was gone, dissipating into the shower's steam. Josh pulled himself into a fetal position, shaking and sobbing. Before losing consciousness, he was aware of someone pounding on the front door, yelling his name.

A dull thud was followed by the splintering of wood as Eric burst into the apartment.

"Josh! Josh! Where are you?" Eric appeared at the bathroom door, wide-eyed and breathing heavily.

Josh was naked and shivering against the tub. He was tangled in the bloody shower curtain. A dark pool gathered on the tile floor beneath him, streaming from multiple cuts and gouges. Steam from the running shower settled over the room like an eerie white blanket.

11

Emergency Physicians Hospital, Room 319

Josh lay completely still. His breathing was artificially rhythmic. His torso held together with gauze and stitches. A thick, plastic tube snaked down his throat draining a pink, watery fluid. A smaller tube funneled oxygen through his nostrils to his damaged brain. His skull had been fractured when he slipped out of the tub, but the doctors had no explanation for the deep claw and bite marks on his back and neck.

Eric slumped in a wooden chair next to the bed, dozing quietly. He had been awake most of the night, watching the blinking equipment monitor Josh's vitals.

The door opened to a nurse cradling a clipboard. She methodically circled Josh, adjusting knobs, checking bandages, and updating her clipboard. She noticed Eric stir.

"Can I get you something?" She smiled politely.

Eric rubbed his eyes and sat up. "Thanks, but I'm fine."

"Well, I'll be here all night if you need anything." She was an attractive, twenty-something, strawberry blonde with bright amethyst eyes.

"Do you think he'll be okay?" Eric asked.

The nurse considered her patient. "I know they're doing all they can. I'm sure he'll be fine." She hesitated, glancing at Josh again. "The bite marks. Was it a dog that did that to him?"

"Couldn't have been a dog," Eric said. "I heard him scream from the landing. When I got to him, he was alone. There was no way out of his apartment except through me, and I didn't see anything."

She stood in awkward silence for a moment before shuffling the papers on her clipboard. "Well, I'm sure he'll be alright." She turned toward the door, not knowing what else to say. "If I can get you anything, just buzz the nurses' station. My name's Mag."

Eric was at a loss. "Thanks," he said, running his fingers through his dark hair. He rested his elbows on his knees and squeezed his eyes shut. He couldn't shake the image of Josh lying on that floor. All the blood. The terror in his eyes.

Eric's front pocket vibrated. He dug his cell phone out and flipped the top back. "Yes?"

A feminine voice sounded concerned on the other end.

"Hey, Sis. Yep, I'm still here. No, there hasn't been any change." He paused while she spoke. "I appreciate that. I'll call you soon."

He folded the phone and slid it back into his pocket. He yawned, stretching his arms over his head, exposing the bottom half of a Celtic cross tattooed on his arm. He stood, lingering a moment over his friend's bed before leaving the room.

Ink & Baud Building

"The Implement is on the move," a man wearing a clerical collar reported optimistically. "We should know something soon." A weak smile betrayed his doubt.

The charcoal suit at the head of the table was unimpressed. He thumbed through a manila folder without looking up. "You're an important man, aren't you, Reverend?" he asked softly. "You have clout in this town. It seems to me, a man with your connections would have no trouble finding a frightened old woman and a little girl."

The Reverend tugged at his constrictive collar. "I can find you another girl," his voice was strained with uncertainty.

The charcoal suit closed the folder and met his eyes. "And I can find another important man."

Cellar Doors

12

Gwen lifted the fork to her mouth and glanced across the table at Jude. The steak was grilled perfectly. Complemented by a smoked paprika marinade, it simply melted in her mouth. Jude had meticulously dressed his kitchen table with a crisp, white tablecloth and a crème candle in the center.

As romantic a dinner as it was, Gwen barely noticed. Her attention was on Jude. He had the worst poker face ever. Actually, that's what she liked most about him. He was too honest to play games; he was an easy read and something was obviously bothering him. She lay her fork down and sipped her raspberry tea.

She remembered their first encounter three months earlier. She was making her morning pit stop at the Coffee Café; he was leaning against the counter in front of her. He butchered the names of three coffee drinks before settling on a caramel macchiato.

"Okay, I'll take a caramel mack-ee-cho-toe," he stammered. Gwen couldn't help but giggle at his complete lack of coffeehouse sophistication. She remembered two things when he turned to see who was making fun of him; his blushing face which grew a shade darker when he saw her, and his sky-blue eyes.

"So, what's going on, Jude?" She cut to the chase.

Jude looked up from his smashed potatoes, realizing he had been swirling them around his plate without taking a bite.

"What do you mean?" Her abruptness caught him off guard. "Nothing's going on."

Gwen waited.

He sighed, leaving his fork standing like a flagpole in the potatoes. "I guess I've just been thinking a lot lately. About you...about us."

Jude met her eyes with his. She was truly breathtaking. Her straight, dark hair had been curled inward just below her bare shoulders. Her soft features and defined cheekbones highlighted her Italian heritage. She wore a black, knee-length Renée Dumarr dinner dress that reminded Jude what an inappropriate choice his Gusset blue jeans and Captain America t-shirt had been.

"I know its only been a couple months, and I really like you..." He stopped mid-sentence and started over. "I mean, I'm not sure how our relationship can continue under the circumstances."

"Circumstances?" she asked.

"With you going to California. I just don't see how a long-distance relationship can work."

"What are you doing, Jude?" Gwen was getting a little agitated. "Like you said, we've only been together three months. And I never said I was for sure taking the job, only that it seemed like a good opportunity. I like spending time with you, and I thought you liked being with me. Isn't that enough for now?"

"Well, yes. I mean, I'm not asking you to marry me or anything. I just don't want you to..." Jude bit his tongue. *Did you really just say that? Idiot.* "What I'm trying to say is..."

A soft chime interrupted his elaboration. "Excuse me," Gwen whispered, pulling a cell phone from her handbag.

Jude could hear a voice bellowing through the earpiece. Gwen didn't speak as she pushed her chair back and stood up, the color draining from her face.

"I'm on my way," she said, disconnecting the call. "There's been an accident at the hospital. I need to go."

13

Emergency Physician Hospital

Gwen and Jude quietly watched the digital numbers climb to the ICU. With a ding, the elevator settled to a stop and the double doors parted to the bustling intensive care unit.

As they stepped out, a police officer met them holding his palms out. "This floor is restricted. Hospital personnel only." The officer motioned them back to the elevator.

"Gwen!" Eric's voice echoed from down the hall.

Gwen peeked over the officer's shoulder. Eric was waving her to the nurses' station. He was flanked by two officers. One nodded permission. As they neared, Gwen noticed the room sectioned off by yellow police tape. A heavyset man, wearing a gray sport coat stepped out scribbling on a notepad. A tall officer with a camera followed closely behind. Gwen felt her stomach knot as Eric approached.

"Thanks for coming so soon, Sis."

"Eric, what happened?" Gwen searched her brother's eyes.

Eric shook his head slowly. "Josh is dead. And I'm not sure what happened yet. I stepped out for some air, and when I got back..." Eric's gaze wandered to the commotion around the crime scene. "I was only gone a few minutes.

"I'm so sorry..." she began.

"I saw his room, Gwen. There's blood everywhere. On the bed, floor, walls. Even splatter marks on the ceiling. The cops don't know anything. I just don't understand how it happened without drawing attention."

Jude cleared his throat, "Maybe it was an accident. Or maybe he had a fight with another patient..." *Stop talking. Shut up.* Jude listened as the words tumbled from his mouth before he could shut it.

Awkward silence stood between them.

"Eric, this is Jude." Gwen's tone was almost apologetic. "He's a friend."

Jude caught the rebuke laced in the introduction, as well as the relationship downgrade. Boyfriend to friend; not a good sign.

"He couldn't move," Eric responded, turning his attention to the crime scene. "He was in a coma."

"Sorry, I didn't know." Jude focused on the floor tiles and bit his lip. He could feel Gwen's cold stare burrowing into his neck.

"What about his family. Do they know?" Gwen asked her brother.

"I don't think so. They haven't had time to contact anyone yet."

Nurse Mag finished her statement with the officers and, seeing Eric, weaved her way toward him. Her eyes were red and puffy.

"I'm so sorry." Remorse clung to each word as she approached.

"It wasn't your fault, Mag."

Mag took Eric's hand in hers. They were damp with sweat. "I feel responsible. I was the last one to check on him, and he was fine. I mean, his condition hadn't changed. But when I came back to log his vitals before my shift ended..." She paused, looking at the police tape. "It was horrible." Her eyes began to well with tears. "I just don't understand."

"It wasn't your fault," Eric repeated, gently squeezing her hand. "You didn't do anything wrong."

The lanky officer with the camera materialized at Jude's elbow. "We have your contact information." He was looking at Eric. "We may have more questions. Until then, you're released to go." He was turning to walk away, then stopped and glanced over his shoulder. "Stay in town," he said as an afterthought.

Mag reached into the front pocket of her smock and pushed her hand into Eric's.

"This is all he came in with. Will you see that it's given to his family?" She turned toward her station, wiping her eyes.

"Of course," Eric said, watching her go.

As the three returned to the elevator, Eric unfolded his fingers revealing a silver necklace. A curled ram's horn reflected the overhead lights.

Cellar Doors

14

Sheriff Roy read the coroner's report a second time before adding it to the top of a stack of papers. He rubbed his eyes and shifted his weight to relieve his aching hip. Time of death was projected to be somewhere between two and four on Friday morning.

The cause of death was reported as *'suffocation by acute thoracic trauma, and blunt aortic injury. The subject's sternum along with six ribs has been fractured, causing extensive pulmonary contusions and internal bleeding.'*

Sheriff Roy hit the speakerphone and dialed the coroner's office. After two rings, a raspy voice answered. "This is Lucas, county coroner…"

"Luke, this is Roy. Listen, I can't read Chinese. Exactly what killed my victim?"

"Hey, Sheriff. Boy, you got yourself an odd one here. Basically, Ted Childs was crushed to death." Roy could hear papers shuffling. "Are you sure you found him in his trailer? The force required to cause this extent of compression to the thoracic cage…well, I've only seen this kind of damage in high-speed accidents where the steering wheel was slammed into the driver's chest." Luke paused to catch his breath. "Or in cases of victims buried under tons of rubble. You sure you're not leaving anything out, Sheriff? Like maybe a tree crashed through the house and mashed this guy or something?"

"Luke, how much pressure would it take to cause that kind of damage? What I'm asking is, could a person generate enough force to do this?"

"What, like using him as a trampoline?" Luke paused a moment. "Maybe, but it would take a lot of concentrated weight. And that would be assuming he was on a hard surface. I don't think you could ground and pound someone to that extent while on a mattress. But even if you could, there would be signs of tissue trauma. External lacerations, bruises, bumps, you know. At least some signs of struggle."

"Let me guess," Sheriff Roy interjected, "he doesn't have any bruises or cuts."

"Not a single hair out of place. Which, in my opinion, rules out an automobile accident." Luke paused again. "So, you think someone dragged this guy off his bed in the middle of the night, stomped him to death, and then put him back in bed?"

"Don't get carried away, Luke. I'm just asking if it's possible."

"Two deaths in two days, Sheriff. What's happening to our little town?"

"I don't know, Luke. What about the kid at the hospital? You had a chance to look at him?"

"There's not much to look at. I've never seen someone torn apart like that. It's almost like an animal got to him. But that's not possible, is it, Sheriff?"

"I don't know, Luke. I don't know anything yet."

15

The setting sun scratched red and violet streaks across the fading skyline. Driving back to Jude's house was quiet. The shock of Josh's murder overshadowed their unfinished conversation. Tragedy seems to have a way of putting things in perspective. Gwen listened to the lonely hum of tires against pavement and picked at the knot of emotions tangled in her heart.

Jude pulled into his driveway, gravel and packed snow snapped under the truck tires.

"I'll start your car." He shifted the truck into park. "Do you want to come in? I can make hot chocolate."

"It's late," she smiled, "I should go. I'm sorry about dinner, you worked so hard to make it perfect. I didn't get a chance to thank you earlier."

She was being cordial, but he detected tension in her voice. He needed to clean up the mess he'd made earlier; clear the awkwardness between them by explaining his true intent. But not tonight. It had been an emotional day, and he had no intention of cramming his foot in his mouth again.

"It's okay. I'm glad you liked it. A rain check then?" was all he managed to mumble, catching a twinkle from her eye.

Was she crying?

He hesitated a moment before reaching for the door handle. *Tell her how you feel. Make it right...* "I'll leave the truck running while I start your car." *Nice going, Captain Compassionate.*

Gwen left his driveway and shifted into 2nd. Her thoughts teetered from her brother and the incident at the hospital to Jude. She had begun to consider him a permanent part of her future. But lately, it seemed he was always speaking when he should be listening. Or vice versa.

Maybe that's what made their dinner conversation so unnerving. A few days ago, she had mentioned a possible job opportunity in California. She probably shouldn't have said anything. But she assumed Jude would be happy for her, and connecting the logical dots, offer to come with her. He didn't have family here, and his editing job could be done wherever he could find a Wi-Fi connection and a post office. Maybe she had been a little too assuming. But what really bothered her was his remark about not being interested in marriage. Maybe she had misjudged his intentions. Was she important to him or just some temporary distraction?

A sudden gust rocked her car, jolting her attention back to the road. Waves of snowflakes drifted through the cone-shaped headlights, covering the road with icy frost. The white fluff scattered and slithered in her wake.

I do like him. But maybe, she thought, just maybe he's not good for me.

16

Eric leaned against his open refrigerator door, staring blankly at nothing in particular. After a moment, he chose the grapefruit juice and held the container against his forehead. Closing his eyes, he tried to silence the barrage of questions that pounded his brain like a jackhammer. His spirit was heavy, and his mind was tired; but he couldn't stop thinking about his dead friend.

In the living room, he dug into his pocket, pulling out a handful of change and the silver necklace. He replayed the last conversation he had with Josh as the pendant reflected the lamplight. If only he had gone straight to Josh's apartment after work. If only he had arrived a few seconds sooner. If only... He dropped the necklace next to his game console and fell into his recliner with a heavy sigh.

Since leaving the hospital, he felt a little off. Out of sorts. His best friend had been killed, which was definitely wreaking havoc with his emotions, but there was something else. He ran his fingers through his hair. Maybe a good night's sleep would help.

Picking himself up from the easy chair, he flipped on the bedroom light and pulled off his shirt. Slowly, he rubbed his shoulder, massaging the stress knots that had bunched up around his neck and triceps. A bold, Celtic cross stretched from the top of his left shoulder down to his elbow. The intricately woven tattoo was dark green against his skin. He shared the same Italian nose and defined cheekbones as Gwen, but he had a square jaw that was usually shaded by two or three days of stubble.

He stretched out on the cool bed allowing the gentle hum from the ceiling fan to unwind his nerves. He was just about to drift off when he sensed something odd. Like the pressure in the room had changed. As he leaned up on his elbows, something in his peripheral vision shifted. The bedroom door creaked slightly then slammed shut with a force that jolted the wall, dropping a framed picture to the floor.

"Who's there!?" Eric jerked up and rolled to the floor, thrusting his right hand between the mattress and box springs.

No answer. His fingers found the metallic outline of his .380 handgun.

"Is someone there?!"

The light bulb dangling from the ceiling fan flickered once and dimmed, as if the power were being drained. Eric's mind raced; he had heard stories of disgruntled vehicle owners taking out their frustration on tow truck operators. But breaking into his house? Unless it was the same person who attacked Josh.

With a fluid motion, he chambered a round and fired two bullets through his closed bedroom door. Both rounds splintered the wood head-high, within inches of each other.

Eric slid around the bed and leaned against the door. He peered through the new peepholes. Other than the strip of blue moonlight that bled through the drapes covering a large picture window, the living room was dark. The moonlight stretched across the floor, over the coffee table and up the far wall. Too much of the room was still in complete darkness; too many places to hide.

The floor creaked, and a chair scraped against tile somewhere in the kitchen. In an instant, Eric jerked the door open and dropped to one knee just inside the living room. He crouched, motionless, allowing his eyes to adjust to the darkness. He steadied his breathing by taking in and expelling a couple of long breaths through his mouth. His ears were still ringing from the gunshots as he held the pistol with both hands in the direction of the creaking floor.

Something clicked to his left. A green circle blinked repeatedly on the face of his Xbox 360 like a fluorescent eye in the darkness. The console's processor whirled to life. *That's not possible*, Eric's mind raced, *consoles can't turn themselves on.*

Movement.

The kitchen floor.

A dark blur bolted from the sink area, squatting low. A chair toppled backward as the shadow passed in front of the refrigerator. Eric squeezed three shots in succession. A two-liter of root beer exploded on the countertop, spraying carbonated syrup up the walls and ceiling. A round slammed into the freezer door, scattering ice cubes across the floor. Another screamed toward the back of the house, splintering glass. Temporarily blinded from the muzzle flash, Eric waved his hand in front of his face, swirling gun smoke. Disoriented, he gripped the pistol and inched backward, away from the kitchen.

A sharp hiss in front of him.

Panic clawed at his gut as the sweet smell of root beer and gunpowder mixed with something else. Something old and decayed. He jerked the trigger blindly and was hit in the stomach. His feet left the floor as he sailed backward over the coffee table. He tensed his muscles, bracing for impact as the gun bucked again in his hand, spewing fire. He felt his body pass through the living room's plate glass window as if he were moving in slow motion. The double-paned panels shattered into daggers around him.

"Oomph!"

The cold earth stopped his descent, slamming the breath from his lungs. Shards of hateful glass showered around him.

Eric rolled to his feet; his gun trained on the gaping hole.

Nothing moved.

He stood shivering in the February night, more from shock than from cold. Warm blood leaked down his arm as he backed away from the window, crunching glass under his bare feet.

He waited a moment, gun pointed at the black hole, expecting his assailant to burst out after him. The only motion was the shredded drapes that swayed lightly in the frigid breeze.

17

K at glanced at her pocket mirror and curled the rebellious pink strand of hair around her ear. Her lime-green eyes looked tired despite her attempt to hide them with smoky eye shadow. She straightened her Movie Mania nametag and tugged the ends of her sleeves over the palms of her hands—a perpetual habit she subconsciously repeated hundreds of times a day.

Luckily, it was cold outside; no one would question her long sleeves. She hated warm weather. All the questions and stares. *"Are you cold? Don't you own a t-shirt?"* She despised the senseless babbling of nosy people. Truthfully, she despised most people in general. She gently scratched her forearm. The heat made the cuts itchy; sweat made them sting.

She folded the mirror and tucked it into her backpack. A handful of patrons roamed between the aisles of rentals; a pack of teenage boys in the game section, a father and son in the new releases, a teenage girl in the romantic comedies.

Kat watched the girl. She was around her age, probably no more than seventeen or eighteen. Blonde curls spilled over her shoulders and tumbled down her back. Kat watched the girl smile as she read the back of a movie jacket.

Pretty.

Innocent.

Alone.

Kat picked up her cell phone and scrolled to her last message. The screen winked to life, revealing a string of digital numbers. She rubbed her forearm a little harder this time. The voices were stirring again.

The blonde girl made her movie selections and placed them on the counter in front of Kat.

"Love the hair," the blonde girl said, flashing a smile.

"Thanks, I did it myself." Kat mimicked her smile as she slid the movies and membership card to her computer.

"Love your outfit; is it Chloé?" Kat pretended to care.

"Oh, gosh no, I could never afford anything like that." The blonde girl blushed. "Actually, found this at the thrift store in the city."

"No kidding." Kat swiped her membership card. "Is your address and phone number current?"

"Oh, yes, we've lived there forever."

"We?" Kat scanned the screen. "It doesn't show any other names on the account."

"My parents have their own," the blonde girl said. "I kept running up late charges, so they made me get my own card. Kinda funny actually, I haven't had a late charge since."

"Parents can be so unfair," Kat said, fighting to maintain her fading smile.

"Tell me about it. They went to Gulf Shores for the week. Didn't even ask if I wanted to go." The blonde girl took her membership card from Kat. "I really don't understand them sometimes."

"Hey, look on the bright side," Kat said, holding up the movie. "Now you can call your boyfriend over for movie night."

"Right. Perfect situation. If only I had a boyfriend." The blonde girl giggled as she pulled her car keys from her handbag. "Have a great day."

"You, too." Kat rubbed her forearm and smiled weakly as the girl pushed through the glass doors. She rolled the phone around in her hand as her eyes followed the blonde girl to her car. The voices swirled to life. She watched her pull out of the parking lot. *People like her don't deserve parents,* the voices whispered. *People like her don't appreciate what they have until it's gone.* Kat's eyes fell to the phone. Maybe the voices were right.

Cellar Doors

18

As Gwen turned the key to her front door, she could hear the phone ringing. Dropping her handbag to the couch, she moved across the room and picked up the receiver. "Hello?"

Static greeted her. "Who's there?" She checked the caller ID. The backlit LED flashed Eric's home phone number. "Eric, are you there?" Gwen raised her voice, trying to speak over the static. The phone clicked twice, disconnecting. Gwen dialed the number and listened to the ringing.

No answer.

Must be a problem with the phone lines, she thought, returning the receiver to the cradle. She walked to the kitchen and noticed a torn sheet of notebook paper held by a grinning sheep magnet. Aunt Gerri's scribbled handwriting noted she would be home late. The phone rang again.

She pulled the receiver to her ear. "Hello?"

Eric's voice was strained. "Gwen, I need to see you. I'm on my way over."

"Eric, what's wrong? Are you all right?" Gwen felt her face flush.

"I'm losing my signal. I'll be there in a few minutes. Stay in—" The call disconnected.

"Eric?!" She screamed at the receiver. The tone of his voice had bordered on panic. She was about to redial when the phone rang again. "Eric, what's going on? What did you mean by 'stay in'?"

Static. The phone number was his home line. She heard movement within the static. Eric couldn't be on the road calling from his cell phone and calling from his home number at the same time.

"Who is this?" She tried to speak with authority, but the fear in her voice betrayed her.

"Look, I don't know who you think you are, but I'm calling the—" The phone clicked dead.

Gwen sat on the couch. Her finger hovered over the 9, trying to decide if she had a good enough reason to bother the police.

Minutes later, a single beam of light played through the living room curtains and slid down the wall. She ran out as Eric clicked off his bike's headlight and leaned into the kickstand.

"Eric?" Gwen realized he was barefoot, wearing boxer shorts and no shirt. His skin was freezing as she grabbed his arm, helping him slide his leg over the seat. She could hear his teeth chattering as he limped from the bike.

"Eric, what happened?!" She noticed dark splotches around his ankles and arm.

He leaned heavily against her, staggering up the steps to the porch, unable to speak. Gwen pushed open the front door and guided him to the living room.

"Lie on the couch, I'll grab some covers." Her voice teetered with controlled panic as she ran to the linen closet.

Eric slid into the corner of the sofa, leaving a crimson streak across the floral pattern. His skin was the color of ash; his body shaking violently in an effort to generate heat. Gwen materialized, heaping blankets on him and rubbing his fingers and hands to jumpstart his circulation and ward off hypothermia.

The phone rang.

Gwen grabbed the receiver by the neck with a frantic, "Who is this?!" Static drowned out her heavy breathing. The caller ID flashed Eric's home number. Gwen slammed the receiver down and picked it up again. Furiously, she jabbed

9-1-1 and waited for a voice. The phone responded with dead silence. No dial tone, no static. Nothing.

Eric moaned from beneath the mountain of blankets, the feeling ebbing back into his frozen limbs.

Gwen dropped the phone and shifted her attention back to her brother who was drifting in and out of consciousness. Trying to speak, his disjointed words made little sense. Twice he jerked into a sitting position, eyes wide with fear, lips forming unspoken syllables. But mostly, his rambling was incoherent, broken sentences. She cleaned and bandaged his feet and arm the best she could and after a time, he settled into a deep sleep. Gwen tried to stay awake, tried to be vigilant. But as the hours dragged, her head nodded, and her eyes surrendered to welcome rest. She nestled into the couch next to her brother and let the familiar fingers of sleep pull her head to her chest. Her nagging anxiety and fear subsided, swirling into blissful numbness as she began to drift away.

A whisper brushed through her mind, *"We are coming."* The voice was soft, but unnatural.

Gwen's body shuddered in apprehension. She opened her eyes, gasping for air, fighting to the surface of her consciousness. The thick haze of sleep slowly gave way to panic. She blinked at the dark room, disoriented. The strange voice still echoed off the walls of her subconscious. She straightened her back and looked at her brother. He was quiet; eyes jerking rapidly under the lids, chest rising and falling in a steady rhythm.

We are coming. The fresh memory played again through her mind. The voice sounded so close—a dream, no doubt, or maybe one of Eric's vocal outbursts. She switched on the floor lamp and shuffled to the kitchen window. The tile was cold on her bare feet, and her neck and shoulders were sore from her odd resting position.

The wall clock showed half past two in the morning. With her fingers, she separated the horizontal blinds facing the driveway. A lone light pole near the outbuilding illuminated the empty space where Aunt Gerri's car was usually parked. She picked up the phone. It was still dead.

Sliding into a kitchen chair, she scolded herself for falling asleep. Her brother was hurt, Aunt Gerri wasn't home, and the phone wasn't working. She considered taking Eric to the hospital. His arm needed attention, but the roads were covered with ice, and she didn't want to chance an accident. *Maybe if I drive slowly I can make it.* She had accidentally left her cell phone in Jude's truck. But Eric had called her from his motorcycle, so his cell phone must still be outside.

The wind picked up, promising another winter storm. A flicker of lightning blinked silently on the horizon. Crooked limbs overlooking the driveway swayed and scratched at the black sky. She cupped her hand against the cool glass pane, leaving a warm outline of her fingertips to slowly evaporate. A chill tingled down her spine as she watched a decayed island of leaves dance circles around the front yard.

I should go get that cell phone.

She walked to the coat closet and pulled Aunt Gerri's goose-down jacket across her shoulders. She glanced at Eric's sleeping form before cracking the door and slipping into the freezing night.

Gwen pulled the jacket around her ears as a jolt of cold blasted away her body heat. As she ducked around the corner of the house to the driveway, she imagined her brother driving his motorcycle in nothing more than boxer shorts. *What could have happened to cause him to act so irrationally?* The wind whipped around the house in brutal waves, taking her breath and stinging her lungs.

Something had been nagging her since leaving the hospital; a premonition of sorts. Something was different about Eric. She was beginning to see cracks in his usually confident demeanor; nicks in his psychological armor. She had always believed nothing could intimidate him; nothing could get to him, as if he were impervious to the flawed nature that plagued the rest of humanity. She had taken comfort in his big brother persona, finding her courage in his confidence. But now, she wondered if she had expected too much. She was beginning to see his human side, his mortality, in all its fallible and feeble weakness. Her big brother was human with very human limitations.

Her fingers responded numbly as she rummaged through the backpack tied to the seat of his motorcycle. Her breath dissipated into white billows of vapor, and her eyes blurred in the stinging wind. Lightning coursed above the tree-line, now followed by the approaching rumble of thunder. Gwen glanced back at the house, coveting the comfort she had left. For a moment, she could make out the silhouette of Eric watching her from the kitchen window. She located the phone and jogged up the porch, twisting the door handle.

The warmth of the house flooded out to greet her. "What are you doing up?" she asked, stepping into the living room. Eric lay motionless, snoring softly on the couch. Her heart skipped with the realization that he had not moved. An eerie sense of foreboding settled on her as she glanced toward the kitchen. No one was there, but that nagging sensation was back; something was very wrong here. She frantically pulled Eric's cell phone from her coat pocket and held the power button down. A dim, amber light flickered before fading out. Dead battery she concluded, or maybe just too cold to work. Her eyes searched the living room and the hallway leading to the back of the house. Her mind was playing tricks on her. She flipped the phone over and pulled the battery off the back, placing it on the nearest floor vent. Soon the furnace would kick on and maybe the heat would thaw the battery out. That's what she hoped, anyway.

From the kitchen, the phone rang. Eric stirred, moaning softly. Gwen jumped at the unexpected noise. "Thank God," she whispered, weaving around the couch to the kitchen countertop.

"Hello?"

Static.

Her heart sank as her eyes fell to the caller ID. Eric's home number blinked back at her. In the static, she could hear movement. Shifting. Breathing.

"We are here..."

The voices were barely audible over the static, but the words were unmistakable.

The phone dropped to the kitchen floor as fear gripped Gwen's throat so tightly she couldn't scream. She backed away, gasping for her next breath. She felt lightheaded, suffocated, like the walls were closing in. Small white dots buzzed around her vision. The room spun as she staggered toward her big brother.

19

Jude pounded on the front door of Gwen's house. He glanced at his wristwatch. It was still a little early, but he really needed to talk to her. He pounded again and was rewarded by the snap of a deadbolt. Eric squinted at the morning light.

"Oh. Eric, it's me, Jude." He said, feeling the awkward need to identify himself. "You remember, Gwen's friend?"

"Right. I remember."

Eric stepped aside allowing him to come in.

"You look pretty rough," Jude nodded at his bandaged arm. "What happened?"

"Feel pretty rough," Eric said. "Someone broke into my place last night; tore my arm up pretty good."

"Who would do that?"

"No idea. It happened so fast, I never really saw anything."

"Is Gwen okay?" Jude's eyes searched the living room.

"She's fine; just exhausted. She was on the floor next to me this morning, so I helped her to bed. I think we both had a pretty rough night."

Jude paused, noticing the blood-stained couch. The severity of the situation began to sink in.

"They attacked you with a knife?"

Eric wrinkled his forehead and slowly unwound the gauze. The skin around the edges was warm to the touch and fiery red. Four jagged cuts started at the top of his left shoulder and ran like plowed rows down to his elbow. They ran the full length of his tattooed cross, as if trying to scratch it out.

Jude made a sour face. "I don't know, maybe you should have that looked at."

"I'm fine," Eric lied, replacing the gauze. "I called the cops. The sheriff's on his way to my house; he wants to get a statement and take a look at the place. Gwen's still asleep. Think you could give me a ride?"

Jude bit his lip. He really needed to talk to Gwen. "Okay, sure."

20

As In Life, Together In Death
Eternally Bound

K at read the dual headstone marking her parents' grave. She imagined her grandmother scrolling through a catalog of flowery quotations before choosing this one. She ran her fingers over the coarse edges and indented letters. Her grandmother had made their resting place feel like a granite Hallmark card. Just random, clichéd drivel. An insensitive platitude lacking the contribution of any emotional investment.

She hated it.

She imagined the advertising agency that wrote it. *No doubt, by some smiling fool in a cubicle. Some socially elite rich boy who had never slept with loss or regret. What right did he have to immortalize my family with his glossy slur of sentimental fodder?* Kat watched tattered clouds creep overhead. And what gave her grandmother the right to make such an important decision without her? Her fingers traced the letters of her daddy's name.

Crows dipped and circled the clouds around her head. Waiting. Staring. Watching her soul.

Kat settled into the niche between the gravestones. It was here, surrounded by still remains and fading memories that she felt most alive. The brightest place in her dark world was here, with her family. But inside, she knew this was a dark place too; the swirling voices were loudest here.

You belong here, Black Kat. And a part of her, perhaps the biggest part, wanted to be here.

Embrace them, Black Kat. Join your family.

Nestled between the headstones of her parents and little brother, she felt near them and yet missed them more than ever. She belonged here. Her wrists throbbed as she curled them around her stomach and shivered in the cold.

Even with her eyes shut, she could see the crows.

21

Jude pulled his Chevy behind the black and white patrol car in front of Eric's house. On the ground below the missing window, a blocky man in a sports coat poked through the glass with a ballpoint pen. He turned to Jude's truck as they climbed out.

"Good morning, gentlemen. I'm Sheriff Roy."

Jude noticed the nametag above the sheriff's gold star: *R. Rodgers.* He smiled to himself. In spite of the circumstances, he found it a little funny the sheriff's name was Roy Rodgers. For a fleeting moment, he considered treating everyone to a cowboy joke.

The sheriff interrupted his bad idea. "You're Eric," Sheriff Roy extended his hand. "I remember reading your statement from the hospital. You and the deceased repossessed cars together, right?"

"For a couple years now," Eric said. "I've been wondering if there's a connection, but I can't imagine who'd do something like that to him, or me."

"No threats from any disgruntled 'clients' that you recall?" the sheriff asked.

"Not really. I mean, people get upset; but nothing serious." Eric watched the sheriff scribble in his notebook. "You think there may be a work connection, don't you? It makes sense. We took some psycho's car, and now he's getting back at us."

Sheriff Roy scratched his chin. "I don't know yet, son." He slid his pen into his front pocket. "Let's have a look inside."

A lanky officer met them at the window. "Front door is locked up tight, Sheriff. No sign of forced entry."

"Unless you count that big hole in front of the house," the sheriff said, giving JD an agitated look.

"The house keys are inside," Eric volunteered. "I didn't exactly have time to gather my things before being thrown out."

Shards of broken glass reflected sunlight like scattered diamonds on the ground. Dried blood was smeared down the windowsill, where it had been absorbed by the drapes.

"You first, JD," the sheriff said, nodding to the deputy.

JD offered the sheriff a 'thanks-a-lot' look before chipping the remaining spikes of glass with his flashlight. He swung a leg over the windowsill and disappeared with a thud inside the dark house. Seconds later, the front door opened.

Sheriff Roy entered first, following the beam of his MagLite. Eric stepped into the house next. His once safe and tranquil home now looked ominous and violated, like a television crime scene. Eric swept his broken home with his eyes; the shock of what happened was replaced with new emotions. Resentment and anger churned in his stomach.

Ice from the freezer had melted to form slippery pools of watered-down root beer. The freezer door stood open, buckled by a single bullet hole.

The sheriff methodically fingered the sharp edges of the entry hole. "You do this?" he looked at Eric.

"Yes," he replied numbly.

The kitchen table had been pushed away from the refrigerator, and the chairs lay on their backs in the root beer soup. The faint scent of gunpowder still clung to the room.

The deputy scanned the floor for evidence, occasionally stooping to peer under furniture with his flashlight. Within minutes, he had retrieved a handful of spent cartridge shells from around the room.

"What happened to your table?" the deputy asked.

Eric stepped around for a better look. He first noticed the red, blinking ring on the face of his Xbox console. Next to the console, under the necklace, the table had been charred.

"That's odd," Eric said under his breath. "That burn mark wasn't there before."

The sheriff took the pen from his pocket and moved the necklace to one side. An outline of it had been burned onto the table.

"Strange," the sheriff grunted, glancing at JD before turning his attention to the bedroom.

He walked through the threshold and stopped at the twin bullet holes in the door. He looked over his shoulder at Eric.

"I did those, too," Eric answered the sheriff's look.

"Nice," the sheriff said, resuming his inspection. "With all this shooting you did, do you think you hit anything besides the refrigerator and door?" Eric caught a hint of sarcasm.

"I don't know. It was dark, but I don't see how I could have missed."

"Did the intruder shoot back?" The sheriff's voice was muffled, like he had his head in the closet.

"No, I didn't see any weapon."

"How many shots did you fire?" The sheriff materialized at the bedroom door again.

"Six, I think. Maybe seven."

"What about the intruder? Do you remember any details at all? Height. Approximate weight. Hair color. Ethnicity. Male, female. Anything?"

"No," Eric replied. "Like I said, it was dark. All I saw was a form. A crouching form. It moved fast and hissed at me."

"Hissed at you, like an animal?" the sheriff asked.

"I guess so, or more like a snake." Eric realized how wild his story was beginning to sound.

"Mmm hmmm." The sheriff stepped back into the living room, scribbling in his notebook.

"One more bullet hole back here, Sheriff," JD called from the laundry room behind the kitchen.

"You said you were hurt?" the sheriff asked Eric, ignoring his deputy.

Eric removed his jacket and peeled back the bandages.

"Well now, that's quite a set of scratches." Sheriff Rodgers winced at the wound. "You better have it looked at."

Eric gingerly pulled his jacket back on. "Look, Sheriff, I know how this is starting to sound. You guys probably think I'm crazy, but I swear I'm telling the truth."

"Son, a few days ago I may have dismissed your little wild west show as a bad drug trip. But after what happened at the hospital, well, let's just say, I don't think you're crazy." He pulled a card from his sports coat. "Call me if you think of anything that might help. We'll keep an eye on things for awhile."

Eric watched the patrol car pull from his driveway. He glanced at the polyester shirt and sweatpants he'd borrowed from his aunt's closet. "Think I'll change clothes and maybe stay with Gwen a couple days," he said, after they had gone. "I can't deal with this right now."

Jude waited in the living room as Eric threw some extra clothes into a bag. He watched the ring on the Xbox silently blink red; the reflection from the pendant winked at him in crimson succession.

"Let's go," Eric said, scooping up the pocket change and necklace with one hand. "Not that it will do any good, but I guess I should lock the front door."

22

Emergency Physicians Hospital

The emergency room was unusually busy. After signing in, Eric and Jude found seats next to a woman with a bandage over her eye. Eric's gaze settled on a sign over the admitting desk: TURN CELL PHONES OFF. "I should let Gwen know where we are."

"I'll give her a call," Jude volunteered, walking toward the automatic doors leading outside. "I'm sure it'll be awhile before they get you in."

"Eric?" A nurse pushing a cart called from the elevators. Her strawberry hair complemented her smile. She left the cart and made her way across the hall.

Eric smiled. "Mag, do you ever leave this place?"

"Guess I could ask you the same thing." Her smile faded to concern. "What happened?"

Eric relayed an abbreviated story as her worried eyes strayed to his arm.

"Looks serious," she whispered. "And you never got a good look at who it was?"

"Never saw a thing," Eric said. "Nothing."

"Sort of like your friend, Josh," Mag pointed out. "I mean, you didn't see anyone in his apartment, either."

Eric shook his head. "I don't know. I've wondered about a connection, but keep coming up blank." He touched his sore arm. "There's something going on here. I just can't figure out why anyone would go to these extremes to..."

Mag's attention was drawn to her vibrating phone. "Listen, Eric," she said, "please call me if there's anything you need." She jotted her number on a prescription sticker. "Meanwhile, I'll see if I can get you in faster. I have a little pull with the emergency room doctors. They owe me for all the Subway and burger runs I make."

"Thanks, Mag, I appreciate your concern."

"I'm serious about calling me," she smiled, returning to her cart.

Eric and Jude left the emergency room with fresh stitches and a prescription to ease the pain.

"Did you talk to Gwen? I really don't like leaving her alone..."

Eric stopped in the middle of his sentence and thrust his hand into his front pocket jerking out the contents. "Hang on a minute, Jude." Stray change bounced off the pavement and rolled away, leaving nothing but the necklace in his grip. "This thing just burned my leg." Eric shook the necklace out of his hand and peeled his fingers open, revealing a rash across his palm.

"Where'd that necklace come from?"

Eric unbuttoned his blue jeans and slid them to his knees. A welt streaked his thigh where the necklace had been cradled in the front pocket.

"It belonged to Josh. I remember him taking it from a car we repossessed."

"I don't understand what just happened," Jude glanced over his shoulder, "but please put your pants back on."

Eric looked sick. "Let me borrow your phone," he said, fastening his jeans and fishing the sheriff's card from his wallet.

23

Gwen waited at the front door as Jude's truck pulled behind her VW. Eric and Jude came in, talking in rapid sentences. Eric tossed the necklace, now wrapped in paper towels, on the kitchen counter next to the phone.

"I'm telling you, there's a connection to the attacks and that necklace," Eric pointed at the discarded pendant. "Josh had it and was attacked; I had it and was attacked. That can't be a coincidence."

"You said it came from a repossessed car. Whose car? Maybe we should just take it back. Get rid of it," Jude said. "Or at least contact the owner. Maybe they can shed some light on this."

Eric thought a moment. "It was in the trailer park, east of town. But what difference would it make if we took it back? You saw what it did to my leg."

"What's going on?" Gwen was tired of being ignored.

"Maybe it's made of magnesium or something. Aren't there types of metals that ignite spontaneously?" Jude asked.

"No, I don't think that's the way it works." Eric said, reaching for the phone. "I'll try the sheriff again; he needs to get over here."

"Someone tell me what's going on!" Gwen's tone stopped the conversation.

Eric noticed Gwen for the first time.

"I'm sorry." Eric wrapped his sister in a tight bear hug. "Thanks for taking care of me last night. I'll make some coffee, and we'll figure this out together."

A pot of Folgers later, they were no closer to making sense of the past few days. Eric scrolled through Wikipedia, waiting for a return call from the sheriff. Gwen and Jude worked together, scrubbing the bloodstain off of the couch.

"Not magnesium," Eric said, clicking the mouse. "Too bulky. It can only ignite if it's shaved into thin slivers."

"Maybe it's just an allergic reaction to the metal in the necklace," Gwen offered.

"Don't think so. It definitely burned me; just like my coffee table. Somehow this thing is generating heat."

"Maybe we should have it tested. Like in a forensics lab." Jude offered.

"Right, Jude. 'Hey guys, could y'all run some special tests on this necklace? Seems it's been attacking the locals.'" Gwen was smiling, but her tone didn't sound like a joke.

Jude studied the sponge in his hand. *My big mouth strikes again. Come on, say something that's actually helpful.* "I guess that does sound a little unbelievable. But, if it's not an allergic reaction or a combustible metal, what does that leave? Jude ventured a glance at Gwen. "I mean, what if it can't be explained that easily?"

"What, you think the necklace is cursed?" Some of the sarcasm drained from Gwen's response.

Jude resumed scrubbing the couch. "I'm just saying."

Gwen considered Jude's idea a moment before changing the subject. "Eric, I'm worried about Aunt Gerri. I haven't heard from her since yesterday and it's just not like her not to check in."

Eric turned his attention from the laptop screen. "I dropped by the Shell station the night Josh was attacked. It was locked up, but I just figured Aunt Gerri shut it down early because of the weather. The roads have been bad. Maybe she's staying with a friend."

"Maybe, but she would have called me." Gwen looked worried. "And there's something else," she lowered her tone.

"I heard voices last night, on the phone. They said they were coming."

"Who said they were coming?" Eric closed the laptop.

Gwen's eyes were vacant, remembering the terror she felt. "I don't know, but they said they were coming here."

"That's it," Eric said, picking up the phone. He punched the sheriff's number again.

Cellar Doors

24

Sheriff Roy Rodgers sat at his cluttered desk sopping up spilled coffee with a restraining order. He shifted weight off his bad hip, causing his leather holster to creak obstinately. He had been elected his last two terms by landslide victories. He joked he was the favored man because of his western name, not his physique. His choice of name had been his father's way of paying homage to his childhood hero and had inadvertently destined Roy to a life in law enforcement—not that he would change anything. He loved serving the community as a peace officer, even though the years had been rough on him.

The small office was busy. The incident at the hospital and the dead guy in a trailer park was more action than Willow had ever seen at once. "And the week's just getting started," he mumbled, dropping the soggy paperwork into the wastebasket.

He picked up a handwritten report, remembering the young man with the injured arm. "Oh, and this guy," he said, glancing again at the paper: *Shot up his house and jumped through a plate glass window.* Roy scratched his sandpaper jowl. "Some kind of crazy has taken over the town," he said, thinking out loud. "Some kind of crazy."

JD poked his head into the office. "Sheriff, that gunslinger from this morning is on the phone again. You know, the one that shot his refrigerator," he said, feeling the need to elaborate.

The sheriff listened to Eric, offering grunts between sentences. After the call, he leaned over until he could see the top of the deputy's head. "JD, ride over and talk to that kid. Says he's got something new to show us."

Deputy JD checked the address the sheriff had given him. He knocked on the door and took a step back, waiting for a response. The door opened, and he recognized the dark-haired gunslinger.

Eric looked over the deputy's shoulder. "Did the sheriff come?" he asked.

"Nope," JD said, glancing at Eric's bandaged arm.

"Sheriff Rodgers told me to come down and take a statement. Said you had new information that might help the investigation."

"Well, yes, but I was hoping to talk to the sheriff personally."

"Look," JD blinked his eyes slowly in obvious agitation. "You're not the only person in this county with a problem. You can give me your statement or wait until we're caught up. Suit yourself." JD turned to leave.

"Hang on," Eric said, "This is important. Just come in."

JD paused in the living room, his eyes memorizing his surroundings. "Is anyone else here?"

"No. My sister and her friend were here, but they went to town."

"Who lives here?" JD glanced at the damp patch on the couch.

"My sister and my aunt," Eric said, feeling a little uncomfortable with the interrogation.

"Sorry," JD apologized, "just a habit. Let's hear this new information you have."

Eric swaddled the necklace in paper towels and held it for JD to take.

"I think this necklace is somehow connected to the attacks on Josh and me." Eric winced at the sound of his claim.

JD glanced at the necklace in Eric's hand, and then at Eric. "You stole someone's necklace and think they killed your friend, and now they're trying to kill you to get it back?" Eric couldn't tell if the deputy was being sarcastic or not.

"No. I mean, I don't know. But there's more," Eric held out his red palm. "It burned me. On my leg, too. At the hospital, it burned through my jeans. Like the charred table at my house."

JD lifted the necklace out of its protective paper towel nest. "Feels cool to me," he said with a slight smile.

Yes. He's making fun of me, Eric decided.

"My sister's been getting some weird phone calls and our aunt is overdue to be home. She hasn't checked in, and we can't reach her."

"Okay," JD said slowly, "have you considered maybe the weird phone calls are your aunt trying to reach you? We've been having some pretty rough electrical storms which will affect cell phone service and the phone lines. I mean, have you considered the obvious?" JD paused for effect. "My guess is your aunt decided to stay an extra day somewhere until the weather cleared and tried to call but couldn't get through. That's my take on it. My advice is to sit tight and chill out until she contacts you. And as for your 'hot' necklace—well, maybe you should give it back to whoever you took it from." JD tossed the necklace to Eric, who slung it to the kitchen counter.

Eric's temper climbed. Obviously, the deputy wasn't taking him seriously. "I didn't call you here for a lecture or your best guess. I'm expecting some actual police help here." Eric tried to remain calm.

JD forced a smile. "Listen, buddy, you've had a rough couple of days. You're tired, injured and obviously under a lot of stress. Relax. Get some rest. Let the Sheriff's Department do its job. And stop calling with these...helpful leads. We'll get to the bottom of your friend's apparent homicide and maybe even figure out how that guy from the trailer park died. But you've got to let the process work."

"What guy from the trailer park?" Eric asked.

JD's face flushed. "Just take my advice and get some rest. I'll talk to the sheriff about having a patrol car spend some time here if you're worried about prank phone calls. That's about all I can do at this point." JD took a step toward the front door.

"The dead guy from the trailer park; he's the same guy we repossessed the car from. Am I right, Deputy?"

"Listen, if something real comes up, call me. But you need to stop pestering the sheriff every time you get a rash or the phone doesn't work. Let us do our job." JD reached for the door handle. "I'll be in touch," he said, letting himself out.

Eric watched him pull the door shut and pause on the porch long enough to light a cigarette before walking to his patrol car.

"Well, that was useless," he mumbled, glancing at the kitchen counter.

The eerie uneasiness was back. Eric rubbed his stitched arm and wondered what to do.

25

"Good afternoon, Leander." Jude and Gwen weaved through the narrow maze of vegetables surrounding the produce peddler.

Leander leaned against the tailgate of his rusty pickup, chomping a purple onion.

"How you doin', buddy?" The old man adjusted his visor to filter the sunshine. He noticed Gwen and smiled. "So, how'd that dinner go?"

"Just fine," Jude cleared his throat, trying to sidestep yet another uncomfortable moment. "Anyway, I know you have a lot of connections in town. We were hoping you might know someone who could help us."

Leander spit a stream of onion juice. "I've been around awhile, seen a lot of faces, hear a lot of stuff. Course, I try to mind my own business. Who is it you're lookin' for?"

"We need to talk to someone who knows about supernatural things."

"Supernatural things?" Leander looked confused.

Jude tried to choose words that wouldn't make him sound like a nut job. "Yeah, like ghosts or haunted jewelry..." Jude stopped, realizing he sounded like a nut job.

Leander bit a chunk out of his onion, staring at the couple as if waiting for the punch line.

"What about the pastor of that big church south of Willow?" Gwen asked, giving Jude a sidelong glance.

"Who, Reverend Ferrell Collins?" Leander shifted his attention to Gwen. "Don't bother talking to Ferrell C; he don't believe in all that Holy Ghost hocus pocus. Besides, I imagine his prayer pipeline is probably a little clogged-up right now. Word is, he's been having after-hours 'confessions' with that young Jessie Belle in the city." Leander bellowed like an old mule at his juicy slice of gossip, scrunching his face into a wad of criss-crossed laugh lines. "The world is full of hypocrites," Leander laughed, "and you can find most of them wearing fancy suits and singin' hymns."

Jude waited as Leander savored his observation with another bite of onion.

"You know what, never mind," Jude said softly. "This was a bad idea. Maybe Eric and the sheriff have come up with something helpful."

Leander furrowed his eyebrows and spit another stream of onion juice. "Ghosts you say? Well, I'll be..." He rolled the cud of onion around his mouth and wiped his nose with a flannel sleeve. He leaned close to Jude. "I may know someone, if you really want to know about things like that." He pulled his sun visor down, casting his face in a green tint.

Jude involuntarily took a step back from the onion aura, his eyes starting to sting.

"We're very serious," Gwen interjected.

Leander lowered his voice. "I got a rental property outside town on Highway 110. The woman who lives there might be able to help you. Her name's Elizabeth LeHan. Think she's one of those weird *one with nature* types." Leander's eyes grew wide. "Kind of a spooky gal, as I recall."

"One with nature," Jude repeated. "Are you saying she's an environmentalist?" He wondered where the conversation had gone wrong. "We're not interested in talking with someone who recycles."

"Think she might be in some sort of cult," Leander said, ignoring Jude again. "Strange woman; she'd buy several bushels of corn and green beans at once. Feeding her cult friends, no doubt. Even thought about kicking her out, but she's got that little girl." He took another bite of onion for emphasis. "Anyway, reckon she might know something about your ghosts."

Jude glanced at Gwen, feeling uncomfortable and a little stupid.

"I'll call Eric and have him meet us there," Gwen offered.

Jude couldn't think of a better option. "What's her address?" he asked reluctantly.

Cellar Doors

26

Ink & Baud Building

The high-backed chair twisted smoothly to face a blinking light on the phone. "Yes?" The voice was smooth, like sand being poured from a paper bag. Recessed lights were dimmed, giving the room a relaxed atmosphere. The subtle hum of Bach drifted from unseen speakers embedded in soundproof walls.

"Good afternoon, Senator." The voice on the other end had a slight mechanical tone; evidence the audio scrambling component was functioning properly.

Every phone conversation was encrypted, every client protected. "Of course," rich laughter resounded off the walls, "we'll work with your schedule as usual."

The phone light blinked dark, and the chair swiveled to meet the others seated around the table. "Three units to Washington tonight." The warm tone had become a monotone whisper, businesslike and crisp. "Blond and male, like before." A manicured hand touched a folder next to the phone. "Has the woman and girl situation been resolved?" The inflection in his voice didn't sound like a question.

"I've made the appropriate arrangements for her return," came a feminine response.

"You realize we've already collected a fee for the unit's delivery? She must be on a plane in two days—undamaged, healthy and clean. Not even a bruise. I hope you understand the importance of these requirements."

"I understand," she replied.

The man didn't look convinced. "What about the Reverend?" His chair twisted back to the phone where a new green light blinked.

"The Reverend has been dismissed."

27

Jude pressed the doorbell and listened to the simultaneous buzz. A few seconds later, the muffled rustle of footsteps creaked toward the front. The heavy maple door opened to reveal a middle-aged woman. Silver strands laced her auburn hair, which was pulled back and held with a transparent clip. She wore a simple cotton pullover and faded blue jeans. Rimless reading glasses framed her sharp hazel eyes that blinked back at them suspiciously.

"Yes?" she asked, her gaze settling on Jude.

Jude cleared his throat, not sure how to start. "Elizabeth LeHan?" he asked awkwardly.

"I'm Beth LeHan," the woman said, "and who are you?"

"My name is Jude. This is Gwen and her brother Eric. We were told you might be able to help us."

"Help you with what?" Beth asked, still holding the door.

Jude noticed her left foot was planted firmly on the backside of the door.

Eric stepped forward, holding out his hand. Wrapped in a wad of paper towels, the silver ram's horn swayed hypnotically at the end of the chain.

"This," Eric stated flatly.

The woman glanced at the pendant, then at Eric holding his eyes with her own. "Where did you get that?" she asked, the door slowly inching closed.

"This may sound crazy," Gwen spoke quickly, "but we think this necklace is somehow responsible for the deaths of two people. We think it's haunted or cursed, and the fruit peddler said you may be able to help us."

Beth hesitated a moment, then opened the door wider. "Come inside," she said, glancing at the necklace again, "but leave that on the porch."

Eric dropped the chain on the swing and followed them into the house.

Jude stepped around an army of open cardboard boxes into a bright living room. Gwen took a seat on the couch facing the hearth. Beth prodded a smoldering log with a poker, sending a parade of orange sparks spiraling up the flue. Jude noticed the mantel held a variety of photos and framed pictures. The predominant centerpiece was a Bible verse in needlepoint:

I will crush all your enemies. I even tell you that I, the LORD, will build a house for you. I Chronicles 17:10

"That's a little more intense than the generic, *Bless this House* motif I've seen," Jude said.

Beth glanced at the mantel and smiled. "Please, have a seat; make yourselves comfortable." She returned the poker to its place. "I have hot tea steeping in the kitchen. I'll bring extra cups, and you can tell me about this problem of yours."

Eric dragged a wooden chair in front of the fireplace and pulled his stocking cap from his head.

Gwen noticed dark streaks soaking through his bandages. He still looked pretty haggard, she thought, as he dropped his head and ran his fingers through his hair.

"There's a good chance this lady will laugh us out of here," Eric spoke up after Beth left the room. "And if she does, I have no idea where to turn next. The sheriff found nothing to go on at my place, nothing to prove I was fighting with anyone other than myself. And after talking with the deputy, I just don't think we should expect much help."

"What did Leander mean when he said Beth could help because she was 'one with nature'?" Gwen asked, trying to find something positive to dwell on.

"Old man Leander is mistaken. He should stick to peddling cabbage and potatoes," Beth smiled, stepping into the living room. She was carrying a tray with four steaming cups. "Communing with nature and dancing under moonlight sounds very cute and whimsical. Our goal was never to commune, but to control." Beth paused over the coffee table. "The old man has confused Wiccan philosophy with something altogether different. I was never a witch."

The room fell uncomfortably silent as she set the tray on the coffee table and removed the sugar bowl's lid.

"Then what exactly are you?" Gwen sounded worried as she accepted a cup from Jude.

Beth seemed to relax. "I'm more than a conqueror, darling, but that's another story. First, tell me how you found your way to my doorstep."

Gwen was the first to speak, relaying the horrific details of the prior few days. Starting with Josh's attack and subsequent death at the hospital, she backtracked to include what little they knew about the pendant.

Eric added his piece to the puzzle, reliving his attack the day the pendant was in his possession. The common thread in each devastating story seemed to be the necklace. Wherever it went, death and destruction followed.

Beth quietly listened, sipping her tea and nodding occasionally.

When Eric finished, she set her cup on the tray and pushed her glasses closer to her eyes.

"I really don't know you kids, and my instinct tells me to ask you to leave. But I know I can't do that. Obviously, you have all been thrust into a world that you know nothing about; and for that, I am sorry." Beth followed the rim of her cup with her finger. "This is truly unfortunate," she said after a moment. "What I'm about to tell you may be hard to understand. I haven't spoken about these things to anyone…" She paused. "Quite honestly, it's a chain in my life that I have broken free from and don't wish to revisit. But, under the circumstances, I believe you need to hear this. The talisman you have is a tool used to exact vengeance; to evoke destruction and death on whomever it is given. It is the calling card of an assassin of sorts. Whoever has it in their possession becomes the target."

"So, you're saying some sort of ninja assassin murdered Josh?" Eric's tone was a little more sarcastic than he intended. "How could someone just stroll into a busy hospital room and murder a patient without being noticed? And what about Josh's apartment?" Eric felt his frustration stir. "There was absolutely no way someone got past me. The windows were locked, and I came through the only door, not to mention his apartment was on the second floor." Eric twisted his cap in his hands and took a deep breath. "I'm sorry," he said finally, "I guess I'm still a little on edge. Having a hard time convincing myself I'm not crazy, and I think maybe I'm starting to lose that argument."

"You're not crazy, Eric," Beth said. "I believe you, and I need to clarify what I meant when I said 'assassin.' The talisman is a beacon that attracts a vicious murderer. But the killer is not a man, woman or even an animal. It is not human."

"A ghost?" Fear laced Gwen's response. "So the necklace *is* haunted?"

"I don't know what your definition of ghost is." Beth smiled weakly. "I don't believe in disembodied spirits floating around looking for bright lights to cross over. I'm talking about a spiritual killer, a roaring lion. A devil."

"Wait a minute. Now you're saying we're being chased by devils?" Eric stood up. "Come on, lady, listen to yourself. I don't believe in haunted jewelry or witches or some pitchfork-toting devil sneaking around killing my friends."

"I suppose you have a more believable explanation?" Beth coolly met Eric's eyes.

The room was quiet as her question hung in the air.

"So, who's responsible for this devil?" Jude asked, breaking the silence.

Beth took a deep breath, hesitating a moment before continuing. "The High Echelon is a close-knit circle of men and women who provide a very specific, rather, a very sinister service. Frankly, the worst form of slave trade you can imagine." Beth nudged her glasses back in place. "Girls within child-bearing years are targeted by the Group. Doesn't matter if they are homeless, runaways or angry teens; they are promised food, shelter, money—whatever it takes to gain their trust. Most women are recruited, but if the Group can't meet the supply with recruitment and bribery, the rules change. They are taken against their will. Stolen from their homes, kidnapped off the streets, picked up from malls or parks. They're collected for the sole purpose of providing a commodity." She paused again, her eyes sad and distant. "They are used to provide offspring; babies that are sold to cult groups and organizations around the world. The babies are harvested to be used in sacrificial rituals."

Gwen felt sick to her stomach. "But why babies?" she asked.

"Primarily, because they are innocent," Beth said. "Pure and untainted by the filth of this world; they're precious. In a sick way, that makes the ritual more poignant. And from a practical sense, newborns are used because they are untraceable. No social security numbers, no birth certificates, and no questions. It's like they never existed. They are nothing more than human fodder used to fuel a demented practice."

"If what you're saying is true, how could something like this happen in a civilized country without someone reporting it? How could our government allow this to happen?" Eric's tone was noticeably softer.

"How could we allow innocent babies to be killed? Is that what you're asking me? Don't be naïve." Beth paused. "Like I said before, the ultimate goal of the Group is power, the same simple lust that has plagued mankind from the beginning. The carnal desire to control others."

Eric studied Beth. "You're part of that Group, aren't you?" It really wasn't a question.

"*Was* part of the Group. I was a Recruiter," she stated, sliding her glasses from her nose and folding them in her lap.

"I found girls who were willing to sell or trade their babies to me. Mostly, I targeted teens and drug addicts, girls who didn't have the guts or money for an abortion or simply saw their child as a bartering chip to feed their chemical addiction." She bowed her head remembering the faces. "So young and so desperate, and I took advantage of them all." She looked around the room. "It's a regret I live with, and will carry until I die."

"What made you change?" Gwen asked.

"Eliana." Beth spoke the name softly. "The little girl I found and was commissioned to keep until it was time."

"Time?"

"She was to be used in a ceremony. She's perfect. Young, spotless. Untraceable. The mistake of a scared teen. I gave her mother thirty dollars and a promise to give her baby a better life. It was a lie, but her mother had no other choice. She was running from her own demons, and I needed a child. I never would have imagined that this little, sin-stained baby would end up stirring hope into my hateful life."

"She has a beautiful name. Where is Eliana now?" Gwen asked.

"She's here, with me." Beth said, smiling. "I took her and ran from the Group. Her name was birthed as a result of my soul-searching cry for help. Her simple faith and trust caused me to consider my own heart; I didn't like what I found." She glanced at the mantel.

Gwen followed her gaze, noticing a handful of photos that captured a smiling, blonde child. She sensed an underlying sadness.

"Eliana's love awakened in me a search for truth," Beth continued. "And I found Someone else who would love me in spite of the horrors I'd committed. The difference was, He not only loved me, but had the ability to forgive my past. I escaped well-deserved condemnation." She blinked back a tear. "So, I took her from the Group about a month ago and have been making arrangements to leave this place forever." She nodded at the boxes on the floor. "Until today, I had hoped we were free from them."

"What do you mean?" Gwen asked.

"That pendant finding its way here is no accident. It was sent to find Eliana and me. Unfortunately, the path it took to find us trampled through your lives first."

"You're saying we brought the devil to you." Gwen's voice was a whisper.

"She's saying we've been used." Eric's face was dark. "Pulled into her sick world, and used to track her and that child."

"I believe so," Beth said apologetically. The demon, or Implement, is not all-knowing. Nor can it be everywhere at once. They set it loose, and it has simply followed a murderous chain of events. There's no telling how many lives have been lost along the way."

"Why didn't you go to the police?" Eric asked with agitation.

A shuffling from the front porch interrupted her response. Eric dashed to the door. The porch swing swayed gently back and forth—the necklace was gone. Beth stepped out of the house, looking across the field of winter rye for any movement. There was nothing. "I think it's time for you to go," she whispered.

Cellar Doors

28

A murder of crows swirled above her head like a disjointed shadow. They settled into the gnarled fingers of the bare oak and squawked at her from their brittle perch.

Kat massaged intensive care lotion between the crevices of her fingers and pulled a final, deep drag from her cigarette. The heavy fog of menthol stung her eyes.

She pushed the lotion under her hoodie sleeve and paused at her wrist.

Fresh, pink lines weaved around rows of white scar tissue. The white ridges marked her skin like braille. She ran her fingers over the scars, reading them like a book. Her eyes wandered to the tree full of crows.

The scars told a sad story.

A child's face flickered to life from a dark place in Kat's soul. She tried to stop the memory, but, like always, it defiantly clawed its way to the surface. She saw the same beautiful face that haunted her sleepless nights. The soft curves of the eyes, the sweet breath, the porcelain cheeks. Fragmented conversations always accompanied the memory. She recognized the gentle laughter and tinges of happiness as her own, but then the emotions became jumbled in her mind. Contentment and happiness succumbed to shame. Innocence to guilt.

Kat realized she was squeezing her wrist. She relaxed her grip, feeling the rush of blood tingle back to her fingertips. She blinked back tears.

She remembered her pregnancy. The butterflies she felt when the test window turned blue. Her first bout with morning sickness, and the excitement of the first wiggle in her belly. She again felt the weight of guilt from keeping the secret from everyone—her parents, her grandmother, even her little brother. She remembered the countless sheets of wadded tissues and notebook paper she piled in the corner of her bedroom. The hours spent trying to find the right words to explain her secret, to ease the disappointment she knew her dad would feel. She couldn't bear the rejection or condemnation. But mostly, she didn't want her dad to be embarrassed of her. She remembered her baggy t-shirts that more than covered her small pooch. And when questioned, blamed her minimal weight gain on teenage hormones and a love/hate relationship with cheese pizza and crème soda.

The baby's father, some nameless boy that she met at the mall, never knew their awkward rendezvous had left him legally responsible. It wasn't really his fault. She had been curious, and he had been available. There was no 'happily ever after' love story to be told.

The automobile accident happened just two days into her second trimester. Her parents and younger brother decided to waste a couple hours at the park; she opted to stay home. Her excuse was a sour stomach, which wasn't far from the truth. She remembered her father kissing her hand before they left. It was his fun way of showing affection. He called her his little frog princess. She cried when he left her room.

Kat's hands began to shake. She brushed aside a tear and searched for another cigarette.

The memories of her life after the accident were cloudy. There was no emotional connection. Just a sequence of events; things just happened. She moved in with her grandmother; a stoic woman of few words and all but stopped going to school. Somewhere in the heartache and hormones, loneliness and regret made a home in her soul. Her secrets grew darker when she discovered the hobby knife in her father's art bag.

She never mentioned her pregnancy, nor did she visit the free clinic. She couldn't handle the shame of being labeled another pregnant teenage statistic. And she couldn't take a chance of anyone finding out about her new obsession with the blade.

The blade became her coping mechanism, a temporary distraction from despair. It was the only thing in her life that helped her feel normal again. She considered it her hateful friend. Her unsettled sleep was plagued by constant nightmares of reaching hands, groping and pulling her baby away.

Even the blade couldn't stop those nightmares.

As she retreated deeper into hopelessness, her demeanor grew dark. Her bright, trendy clothes were replaced with moody-colored hoodies and muted long-sleeved shirts. Summer fashion just couldn't hide the marks anymore. Her shoulder-length, dishwater blonde hair was cropped and dyed black. In her effort to disappear, she stuck out more.

Kat remembered the only outfit she ever bought for her baby: a red onesie with a laughing Elmo. It had short sleeves. She kept it tucked under the mattress in her room. Some nights she would use it to stifle her crying, other nights to wipe the blood from her razor. Most nights, she just held it to her chest and wondered if the pain would ever stop.

She watched the crows; they screamed at her. Their hateful eyes dissecting and exposing her soul. They could see inside of her; they knew her secrets. And they blamed her. She dropped her eyes in shame as their vocal accusations continued. She had done evil things. Unspeakable things.

Cellar Doors

29

Reverend Ferrell Collins stumbled down the stairwell. His hard-soled loafers clapped against the metal steps, echoing down the hollow spiral. His breathing was a forced wheeze. Sweat followed etched lines down his face, soaking his clerical collar. He clutched his stomach and swayed near the edge of the railing, swallowing against the sudden feeling of vertigo. The stairwell wound down three stories to a poorly lit cement floor.

A jagged line soaked through his shirt, staining his fingers. He stopped on the second floor landing and rested against the metal rail. His breath came in quick, shallow gulps, like a woman in labor.

He shot a glance up the stairwell before continuing his descent to the bottom. On the ground floor, he caught his breath and fell into the exit door. The night air bit his face. He cursed through clenched teeth as his legs buckled, slamming him against the building. The wicked streak on his gut grew, soaking a patch the size of a football above his belt. His face drained to the color of ash in the half-moonlight.

He was aware of the night sounds. The subtle buzz of the streetlights, the gust of wind that hurried fallen leaves down the sidewalk. The scratching of a street sweeper echoing from a nearby alley.

The city was sleeping.

Ferrell pushed himself from the building, leaving a wet smudge on the crypt-colored bricks. He winced and guided himself toward a parking lot across the street. Crossing beneath sodium lights, he plowed through an ivy hedge that separated the sidewalk from the parking area.

Behind him, the door swung open again, clanging against the bricks. Ferrell's mind screamed to hurry, but the loss of blood slowed his reflexes to a limp. He shot a glance over his shoulder before searching through the shadowed rows of cars. "Where is it...?" His voice was shaky.

He caught his breath and pushed himself toward the nearest row. A reflective Chaplain sticker beckoned to him from the Camry on the end. Dark streaks marred the cars he touched, coloring his movement in crimson. He reached his car and rested on the bumper. Holding his breath, he dug into his pocket, searching for keys.

The pain had become nearly unbearable as he took a short breath and closed his eyes, trying to steady his hands before checking his other pocket. His wristwatch and wallet were missing too, but he knew this wasn't some random mugging.

Across the street, a shadow separated from the hotel and slid down the sidewalk, crossing the street near the parking lot.

Ferrell searched the street behind him; someone was there. Prowling just out of sight.

Watching him.

Tracking him.

He stumbled away from his car with renewed determination. A sticky rivulet of blood slid down his leg and bubbled over his loafers, leaving sole marks on the stone walkway.

On the far side of the parking lot, an unfinished marble fountain was circled by orange construction cones. Twin baby cherubim topped the fountain; their stone mouths were dark holes, their pupilless eyes lifted in reverence. Leaning against the empty reservoir, he groaned and slid to the ground. Gingerly, he pulled apart the bottom buttons of his shirt, exposing a freshly stitched gash across his abdomen. Bright blood seeped from criss-crossed sutures. The stitch job looked hurried, uneven and very unprofessional. His heart thumped faster, pumping streams of blood from the wound. Ferrell squeezed his eyes shut and dropped his head. Panic was killing him.

What have they done to me?

There was no doubt who was responsible. The High Echelon wasn't satisfied with his progress. *Couldn't have taken my kidneys, or any other important organ. I never would have made it this far.*

He tried piecing together what had happened. His last memory was driving to the city. Jessie had called and needed to see him desperately. He remembered parking his car, locking the door...and then, nothing. He awoke on the floor of a hotel room in a pool of blood. For a moment, he considered going back to the hotel for help. *But what if they're still there?* He searched the shadows around him. *And somebody's still following me.*

Panic jolted his blood pressure a few notches higher.

"But, if they were going to kill me, they would have done it by now."

But still, the doubts whispered. *What if this is the end? What if I don't make it? No one would know to look for me.* Barb was speaking at a women's conference in Minnesota. She wouldn't be home for another three days. No one else would miss him until Sunday, when he was expected to lead his flock from the pulpit. His nerves began to unravel.

He remembered the last meeting with the Group. They commissioned him to find the woman and the child. But the High Echelon was impatient, expecting miracles from him. Even with connections through the church, it wasn't easy finding people who didn't want to be found. He needed more time. The Implement had been released to hunt them down, but Ferrell didn't like the idea of using it. Demons were crude and couldn't be controlled, only redirected—and even then, couldn't be trusted.

Ferrell wiped sticky fingers on his slacks. "I'll sort out this misunderstanding; talk to the Group and explain I'm doing all I can. Then find the runaway Recruiter and the stolen girl." *Just a little more time is all I need. They'll understand. This is just their way of making a point; driving home the seriousness of the situation. They won't do anything drastic.*

"They need me," he assured himself. "I'm an important man."

But doubt and panic chipped away at his argument.

A new thought brushed through his soul: *What about God? Maybe He can save me. Maybe it's not too late to ask for help.*

Ferrell shook his head, attempting to clear the clutter. Weak people cry for God when trouble comes, he reasoned. They turn to fairytales when they can't handle reality. "Well, I'm not a weak man." His voice was becoming hoarse. "Nor do I believe in fairytales."

The front of his shirt was now completely saturated. "What could they have taken out of me?" His voice was garbled and distant in his ears.

Beyond the fountain, a small park nestled between a cluster of tall buildings. Topping one of the buildings, Ferrell recognized the faint outline of a glowing red cross. The clinic was no more than five hundred yards through the park.

"I can make that," he said, coughing up a mouthful of blood.

A breath of cold air rattled through black tree limbs. Ferrell trudged halfway through the park when a bolt of pain crumpled him to his knees. His heart hammered in his chest, pumping his life out by the cupful. His vision blurred as he gripped his gut, trying to dam the bloody leak. The Red Cross was just a little farther.

"A few more steps," he said. "Just a little farther." A hint of pride seasoned his determination. He searched the shadows around him. "You monsters didn't beat me!" He lifted his eyes to the stars. "And I didn't need You to save me."

Ferrell C. had overseen the largest congregation in the county for fifteen years. But deep inside, he knew there was no God. No omnipotent Knight in shining armor bent on sweeping His Bride away from a world in chaos. No sweet by-and-by when we die. God was nothing more than a conjured projection of human superstition and weakness. A clever bedtime story you tell children to lull them to sleep or make them behave. God was like the bogeyman. Ferrell's mind began to unravel.

Maybe God *was* the bogeyman.

He glared at the cold sky, the dark trees, the distant city lights that blinked back without regard.

"I don't need You now." He pushed himself to his feet and shuffled to his glowing red salvation. "And I never will."

A shadow separated from the water fountain, clicking and scratching the cool stones. Razor-thin, yellow eyes locked on the man as he struggled across the park.

Ferrell edged into the perimeter of the cross' crimson glow when the burning sensation blossomed in his gut. The agitation grew more intense with each step. He stopped to compose himself. The burning became more and more unbearable, spreading over his chest, to his liver and around to his kidneys. He swayed under the glowing cross and dropped to his knees. The smell of burning flesh rose from his shirt.

He ripped the shirt's buttons apart, confused by the dark patch spreading across his chest.

He was burning.

Literally.

Disbelief gave way to gut-wrenching pain, and he screamed. His body lurched and heaved, forcing him to his back. He convulsed and writhed in the mud. Through the agony, he could see the laceration on his gut radiate bright red, incandescent under the skin. He screamed from the depths of his soul, clawing at the wound.

The wind picked up and whipped around him, catching and muffling his tortured howl.

Ferrell thrashed and wallowed in the widening pool of blood and mud, gnashing his teeth. He jerked himself into a sitting position, digging at the wound, popping the sutures. The gash sagged open. Flesh glistened in the crimson light of the Red Cross. A wisp of smoke curled from the wound.

The demon fell on Ferrell like a hungry tide. Tearing at his clothes, ripping and digging into his stomach. Ferrell felt his burning entrails being jerked free. He choked on a spurt of blood as the demon pulled something from the cavity. It reflected the monster's yellow eyes.

A metallic twinkle.

A necklace. Ferrell's eyes rolled back in his skull. They had sewn the talisman inside of him intending for the demon to retrieve it. Random questions shot through his mind, but one question screamed louder than the others. Only one question truly held any significance. One last moment of clarity.

What about God?

As his lifeblood soaked into the frozen earth, Reverend Ferrell Collins faced the answer alone.

30

J udas smiled with dark eyes. From the safety of the parking lot, he watched the reverend meet his Maker.

"Well now, that had to hurt," he chuckled, flipping a smoldering cigarette toward the fountain. Ferrell had grown complacent and arrogant. He let his seat on the High Echelon go to his head. Judas watched the shadow detach itself from the mangled body.

It was watching him.

He took a couple steps back, giving the demon plenty of space. He would never make the mistake of turning his back to it again.

It had been Ferrell's responsibility to find the woman and the girl. He had failed. And the Group didn't take failure lightly.

They ordered Judas to handle the situation. Unfortunately for the Reverend, that didn't include a stern lecture and a second chance. Judas moved closer to the grisly scene; the Implement had scattered Ferrell's intestines, and left the talisman across his face. *Actually, with Ferrell out of the way, I'll be on my way to their good graces a little faster.* He considered the disemboweled preacher on the ground. "Oh yes, Reverend, I believe your unfortunate circumstance will definitely work to my advantage."

He raised his eyes to the glowing red cross and grinned at his cleverness. His cell phone vibrated in his coat pocket.

"Judas, do you know who this is?" The feminine voice was filtered with an electronic component. He recognized the digital scrambler cycling in the background. The High Echelon was anything but subtle.

"Telemarketer?" he smiled.

"Judas, you have twelve hours to find that child. If she's not delivered, I fear things could get very complicated for you."

"Oh my. How awful for me." Judas continued to grin at the phone.

"I fear you're not giving the seriousness of this situation your full attention, Judas."

"Seems you fear a lot of things."

Silence.

"Tell our friends to relax." Judas breathed into the receiver. "I'll find the pretty little girl. I'll even drop her by your house if you like. Now, what was your address again?"

"Twelve hours, Judas." <Click.>

Judas searched the shadows. The Implement was gone. He retrieved the necklace and left the body to be discovered by early morning joggers.

Back in his Chevy, he hung the necklace from his rearview mirror and watched it sway as he considered his next move.

31

Gwen bent the horizontal blinds, checking the driveway. It was dusk, and a county sheriff's car had pulled just outside the light pole. A wisp of exhaust curled from the muffler. She recognized the flicker of a cigarette lighter in the driver's seat.

The visit with Beth had unnerved her, but she felt a little better knowing the police were close. She was worried about Aunt Gerri. She glanced at the phone; it had been a full two days. And now, Aunt Gerri's cell was skipping straight to voice-mail. She reached for the receiver again.

The phone rang.

Gwen jerked her hand away; her heart pounding as a rush of adrenaline surged through her body. It rang a second time. She glanced at the window—the police were nearby, she assured herself. Maybe it was Aunt Gerri. She picked up the receiver on the third ring and held her breath. "Hello?"

"Gwen? Hi, this is Mag from the hospital. I'm sorry to bother you; I'm actually looking for Eric."

"Oh, hi," she said, relieved. "Eric's not here right now."

"I'm sorry, I was just concerned about his arm. It looked pretty bad. I tried calling his cell but haven't had any luck getting through."

Gwen glanced at the floor register, remembering Eric's thawing cell phone battery. "Yes, he doesn't have his phone with him right now, but I'll tell him you called when I see him."

"Will you see him tonight?" Mag asked.

"Not sure. I think he's boarding up his broken window."

"Oh, just let him know I asked about him. Sorry again to bother you."

"No, it's no bother," Gwen replied. "I'll tell him."

"Thanks, see you soon." Mag said, hanging up.

Gwen dialed her aunt's number again. Still no answer. She left another message. Feeling a little more at ease, she took a deep breath and opened the kitchen pantry, deciding on a packet of ramen noodles.

She didn't notice the tall figure standing across her living room in the hallway.

32

Kat sat in the park beneath her oak and watched the sky color itself in shades of rose. Above her, the crows swayed on the tree's sharp fingers.

Watching her.

She remembered the last week of her pregnancy. She was tired and scared, but there was no one to turn to because nobody knew. She wondered what would happen when the time to deliver came.

Would she be the despised girl on the five o'clock news who gave birth in a public restroom? Or the bad mother who left her baby in a back-alley dumpster? How could she explain the sudden appearance of a baby to her grandmother? She certainly couldn't take it to school, nor could she leave it home locked in her room.

Panic and fear swirled around her. She could run away, but what would that help? She carried her shame with her.

She remembered the hopeless, trapped feeling as she sat in the mall's food court while watching the pretty teenagers drift by; a colorful blur of giggles and excitement. They would gossip behind nail-polished fingers and complain of overbearing parents. Rave about shoes and hairstyles while swooning over boys.

Kat would listen to their random babbling and seethe. They had no idea how claustrophobic heartache and despair could be, no clue how dark and lonely the bottom really was. They had no idea the price she would gladly pay to see her family alive again. She hated them all. And she began to notice other voices. Her thoughts seemed to take on a life of their own.

Kat recalled the woman with hazel eyes. They reminded Kat of her mother's: gentle, with calculated intelligence. She was older, probably fifty or sixty, with an almost grandmotherly charm. She noticed the woman watching her from a kiosk near the food court; she didn't know how long she had been there.

Finally, she came to Kat's table and sat down. "How far along are you?" the woman asked.

Kat's mind fumbled for a response. "What do you mean?" she asked weakly.

"You're pregnant. How far along are you?" There was no accusation in her voice, just a simple question.

Kat remembered tugging the hoodie over her stomach and feeling her shoulders tense. She glanced around the food court, looking for the nearest exit.

"It's okay, dear." The woman smiled, noticing Kat's apprehension. "I'm not going to say anything to anyone…"

The crows flapped from the tangled limbs in a great commotion; blurry splotches in the raspberry sky. Kat watched their spindly wings rise and dip. They screamed at her over their glossy black shoulders. Taunting and cackling.

Kat remembered sitting in her room, holding the red onesie. She remembered the emptiness in her soul and the emptiness in her womb. No more gentle kicking or soft strumming. Her hands shook slightly as she meticulously slit the letter 'L' from Elmo's name. Now the tattered and bloodstained onesie reflected a more accurate description of her emotionally wrecked life. Her vacant eyes reflected the glint of the razor.

The woman had promised a safe and happy life for her baby; a good family to love and cherish the child. She made all the arrangements for the delivery. There were no forms to fill out, no questions, no prying eyes. No blame.

Kat was given thirty dollars and the woman's phone number. She used the thirty dollars to add a pink streak to her black hair. A pink strand in remembrance of a daughter she would never hold. She used the phone number to call the woman when her nights were especially dark. The woman's soft voice would help ease the guilt of her decision, temporarily holding at bay the voices that now taunted Kat constantly. Voices that reminded her of the evil things she had done. The unspeakable things. The voices teased that her baby was gone forever. And deep inside, she knew the voices were right.

Kat waited until the crows were gone before slipping to the base of the oak tree. Her fingers traced the three small crosses that she had etched in the bark. Under the crosses was a small heart. Her fingers lingered over the heart for a moment as she caressed the memory of her baby. She turned to go, a wispy shadow of a girl unnoticed in the bustle of life.

Cellar Doors

33

Gwen snipped the packet of noodles with her kitchen scissors. Her hands were trembling. She needed to rest; needed to stop thinking for a while. But she just couldn't shift her brain into neutral.

Recent events tumbled through her memory like rows of dominoes. The hospital room with blood on the walls. The police tape. The ringing phone. The gashes on Eric's arm. The little girl on the mantel. She shuddered at the idea of an underlying supernatural web connecting the events together and tried focusing on the pot of boiling water. She needed to feel normal. She would eat, shower and get some sleep. Her mind began the cycle again.

Jude. Now, there was box of emotions she was just not ready to unpack...

Something was wrong. Something besides her tangled thoughts and emotions. She suddenly felt a nagging sense of urgency. A feeling that something was out of place. Like the pressure in the room had changed. A feeling that she was not alone...She turned.

A blur passed in front of her face. A sharp prick below her shoulder. She pushed away from the counter, fighting against the arm that had snaked around her neck. Squeezing.

"Still! Hold still," a voice hissed in her ear. "Don't fight us!"

Gwen blindly jabbed the scissors at her attacker hoping to free herself.

A warm sensation spread from her shoulder, creeping down her legs and up her neck.

Her mind screamed warnings, but her body was unable to respond.

The drug seeped through her system, shutting it down like office lights in a skyscraper. She dropped to the floor. Unable to move; unable to feel anything but the warmth that crawled over her head, tingling her lips. Her vision began to fade as she watched the kitchen light swing rhythmically on the ceiling. It doubled, becoming two lights. Then one light. Then two lights. A face leaned over her.

"We told you we were here."

She couldn't speak, but she recognized the voice, the face. A tinge of shock registered before she drifted away.

But I trusted you...

34

Eric pulled his Kawasaki up to Gwen's house. Jude's truck idled in the driveway. A soft chime announced the driver's side door was still open. Something was wrong. Walking up the steps he found the front door standing open. He pushed his way in. Jude was standing at the kitchen counter.

"What's going on, Jude? And what happened to your face?

Jude's finger drifted to a small cut on his cheek. "Shaving mishap. It's nothing."

"Where's Gwen?"

"I don't know," Jude stammered. "I just got here. The door was open, and this was on the counter next to the phone." Jude handed a folded paper to Eric.

BRING MY PROPERTY:
40°15'8"N 58°26'23"E
CELLAR DOORS

"What property?" Eric's voice was strained as he slowly read the demand again.

"It's them, Eric; it has to be them. The Group Beth told us about."

"Where's Gwen, Jude? Where's my sister?"

"I don't know, Eric."

"I'm calling the sheriff," Eric stated flatly, reaching for the phone.

"Wait, we need to think this through." Jude grabbed Eric's arm.

"We don't know who to trust. I mean, the cops haven't been exactly helpful up to this point. Wasn't there supposed to be an officer watching Gwen last night? Where is he? Where's the cop, Eric?" Jude's voice climbed in desperation as he spoke.

"Maybe they got him, too. I won't stand here while my sister's out there somewhere," Eric said quietly through clenched teeth. "I'm going to find her." Eric scooped up his cell phone battery from the floor register and attached it to the back of his phone.

"Okay. Look, Eric, I agree. We go get her. Assuming that's where she is." Jude pointed at the paper. "But we need a better plan than just barging into a situation that could get Gwen hurt. Listen to me, if they were going to harm her, why bother taking her? If Eliana is the property they're demanding, then maybe Gwen is the bargaining chip they intend to use."

"Do what you want, Jude," Eric said. " I don't care about that little girl, the cops or you. I'm going to find my sister." He stormed out the front door without looking back.

The phone on the counter rang.

35

Gwen awoke to the sound of sobbing. A child's whimper. The small voice rose and fell like a mournful tide resonating from somewhere near, or far; she couldn't judge the distance. She opened her eyes to complete darkness. She was lying on her back on what felt like a damp, stone floor.

Her flannel pj's were soaking wet and plastered to her body with a slimy layer of mud. The musty smell of mildew and earth mixed with something else. A hint of spoiled meat.

She rolled to her knees and waved a hand in front of her face, brushing away what felt like curtains of dangling spider webs. Slowly, she crawled forward, keeping one hand in front of her face as she groped for a wall. Her head throbbed in painful waves, and her movement was sluggish—aftereffects of the drug, she reasoned.

"Hello?" she whispered, not sure she really wanted to be heard.

The darkness was thick and bone-chilling. Gwen's fingers found a wall, and she lifted herself off her knees to her feet. Mud slid between her toes as she shuffled blindly along the perimeter toward the sound of weeping.

Her fingers traced the outline of the cavern, searching for something, anything familiar. She found the surface was riddled with sharp crevices and pockets. Wispy tentacles brushed against her fingers and hands. She imagined nests of millipedes and spiders prodding with outstretched legs and fangs. Reaching to pull her into their prickly fissures.

"Please, can anyone hear me?" She spoke louder to the darkness.

The sobbing stopped. Gwen heard a faint rustling and the muffled sound of a door shifting on hinges. She quickened her pace, moving in the direction of the sound. "Please!" her voice echoed around her.

Her fingers brushed against coarse fur. A flurry of movement and flapping sent Gwen flailing backward in the mud. She landed hard on her tailbone as a startled bat screeched overhead.

Gwen rolled to her side, holding her lower back. She was trying to be strong. Trying to be levelheaded.

Trying not to cry.

But as she shivered in the cold mud and darkness, the gravity of her situation pushed her emotions to the surface. She was alone in this dark place and no one knew where she was, not even her.

Tears bubbled from deep inside and spilled down her face. Pulling her knees to her chest, she closed her eyes and gently rocked back and forth. For as long as she could remember, she had been afraid. Afraid of the dark, afraid of rejection. Afraid of being alone. Over time, she had learned to suppress her demons by smothering them with borrowed self-confidence and faith in others. But now, they were creeping their way out of the shadows of her soul. Toppling her frail walls and breaching her stronghold.

Gwen hugged her knees tightly and wept. The child's sobbing somewhere beyond her own private hell, began again. It mingled with her own soft whimpering. The mournful noise created a soft choir of anguish that drifted and permeated her dark prison.

36

Eric leaned his motorcycle in front of his house and dialed Beth's number. It was time for answers, not a bunch of ghost stories and superstitions.

A generic answering machine voice instructed him to leave a message.

Eric tapped the speakerphone and slid off his Kawasaki. "Beth, this is Eric. We need to talk."

The phone clicked. "Eric? What's going on?"

Eric skipped the small talk. "Gwen's been taken. Sometime last night she was taken."

"Jesus, help us."

"I need to know who these people are, Beth."

The line was quiet.

"Beth, did you hear me? Gwen's gone!"

Her voice was small when she answered. "I don't know where they would take her, Eric. And I'm sorry, but I don't know who they are."

"How could you not know the very people who sent you on your twisted errands?" Eric looked incredulously at his cell phone. "You don't have a name or an address? Anything at all?"

"You don't understand the secret nature of the Group," Beth said, collecting her thoughts. "The High Echelon is very distrustful of everyone, including itself."

Eric took a deep breath. "Beth, tell me everything you know. Don't hold any information back, no matter how insignificant you think it is. There must be something that can help me find my sister."

"I'll tell you what little I know about them, Eric, but I don't think it will help. Hold on," she said.

Eric heard the receiver bump against a table and a door click shut. Beth retrieved the receiver and cleared her throat.

"The High Echelon is a global community broken down into geographical divisions, or Chapters. Each Chapter is overseen by a Six-Seat Hierarchy. The Six Seats of each Chapter govern a number of Recruiters, Surrogates, Taskmasters and Implements."

Eric could sense the distress in her voice as she dug through buried memories. "I remember you telling us you were a Recruiter, but what's a Taskmaster and Implement?"

Beth paused, allowing vivid memories to surface. "Recruiters and Implements are controlled by the Taskmaster. The Implement is the assassin."

"You mean the ghost," Eric said, without attempting to hide his skepticism.

She ignored or didn't hear his tone. "Yes, the Implement is the demon charged to carry out each Chapter's will. Usually a token or talisman is used to direct the spirit, but not always. Some are loosed to kill without discretion." Beth's voice was strained.

Eric changed the subject. "So, you don't know any of these 'six seats' people?"

"No," Beth said. "For the Group's self-preservation, they never gave real names or personal phone numbers. The information we were given was very limited. The Six Seats know us, but we don't know them. Only they make contact. The idea of being damaged from within is the only thing they fear.

The Group has enough political influence not to be concerned with local law enforcement, but is extremely apprehensive of its own self-destruction. It fears betrayal from within. Or, in my case, dissension if a member loses heart. Everything they do is for the ultimate protection of the Group."

"So, how did they contact you?"

"Technologically, they are very advanced. They use encrypted radio waves."

"They communicate to you through your radio?"

"Not exactly." She noticed the skepticism this time. "I was implanted with an RFGP chip. The Biochip would filter encrypted messages to my cell phone. As long as I had my phone within a few inches of the chip, I could read the text messages they sent."

"Encrypted Biochips? Who are these people?"

"The chip is small, about the size of a grain of rice. It was embedded under the skin of my right wrist."

"*Was* embedded?" The skepticism was gone.

"I removed it when I took Eliana and left. I assumed they had the capacity to track it so I threw away the phone and moved. But I still have my Taskmaster's number. His name is Judas. He would text me with the number of units, I mean, women or children that were needed.

"You never had personal contact with him?" Eric asked.

"No, I've never seen him, nor have I heard his voice without it being encrypted." Her tone was distant. "You asked me before why I didn't go to the police, I hope you understand my reason now. I didn't know who I could trust. I still don't know who they are or how much influence they have. I don't deny that I deserve to be punished for my involvement with these monsters, and I will gladly take responsibility for my actions. But Eliana is innocent, and I can't allow these evil people to find her."

Eric swallowed hard. "I've contacted the Sheriff's Department," he said. "I hope I haven't made a mistake."

Beth paused. "How well do you know Jude?"

"Jude, Gwen's boyfriend? I met him the other day. Why?" Eric sounded confused.

"I'm sorry. I don't mean to insinuate; maybe it's just the name association," Beth explained. "Within the Group, we were given new names; new identities. They said it was for our protection, but I think giving us an alter ego was a psychological means of helping to cope with the guilty emotions attached to what we did."

"What do you mean?"

"Being able to blame someone else for the horrible things I did helped justify my actions. I created another personality to shift guilt."

"The whole *devil made me do it* scenario, huh?" Eric asked.

"Something like that," Beth said. "I guess I have trust issues now. Even with myself."

"I think I understand," Eric said. "You think Jude may be your contact, Judas. But you're wrong. Gwen's spent a lot of time with him. She'll vouch for Jude. He's one of the good guys."

"And now Gwen's gone," Beth pointed out.

"You said you have his number?" Eric changed the subject.

"Yes," Beth said, "but what are you going to do?"

"If I find Judas, I find my sister."

"I don't recommend doing that, Eric. You're tampering with powers that you can't physically or spiritually handle." Beth held the phone closer to her mouth and lowered her voice. "The demon tried to kill you once, it may succeed next time." She paused. "You're not wrestling against flesh and blood."

"Get yourself and Eliana to safety," Eric said. "I can handle myself."

Moments later, Jude's cell phone vibrated; he glanced at the number without answering. "Interesting," he said under his breath. "Believe it's time I dropped in on Elizabeth again."

37

E ric paused at his back door. His reflection in the glass showed a tired man. Dark rings circled his eyes like coffee stains. He felt like he had aged a decade in the last few days. Stepping into the kitchen, he was greeted by the smell of spoiled groceries.

He made his way to the bedroom and pulled a portable GPS out of a box in the closet. He checked to see if the batteries were still good. Satisfied, he grabbed his gun and a box of .380 shells and stuffed them into his pocket.

He stood quietly at the foot of his bed remembering the attack. The chilling hiss. The fear. The same uneasiness bristled his skin as he rubbed his clawed arm. It was tingling again as he stepped into the kitchen.

"Eric?"

Mag stood at the back door.

"Eric, I've been worried about you." The morning sun outlined her crimson hair like a fiery halo.

"Mag," Eric started, a little surprised to see her. "What are you doing here?"

"I've been calling your number all day; I was worried. Afraid something had happened to you, too." she said.

"I'm sorry, it's just been a little crazy lately. I haven't had time to check my phone messages with everything going on. But I'm okay. Really."

"Have you seen yourself?" She stepped closer, touching his hand. "You really don't look that 'okay.' I told you to call if you needed anything, remember?"

Eric's mood softened as he rubbed his stubbled chin, remembering how bad he really looked. "Like I said, it's been a crazy couple of days."

"Tell me," she was closer now. Something about her voice, or was it her eyes? They glowed a soft lavender.

"I know I don't have the right to be here, but I was so worried."

"Mag, I appreciate your concern, but I'm really in a hurry..."

"Please, I just want to help." Her arms slid around him. Her breath was warm on his neck. "Let me help." Her lips brushed his mouth, pressing closer.

Eric closed his eyes and drank in the moment. His fingers slid through her hair, resting at the base of her neck.

It helped.

38

Jude rapped on the heavy maple door for the second time, and heard the muffled voice of Eliana call for Beth. He waited while she snapped the dead bolt with her tiny fingers. A frigid breeze sent packing paper scurrying through the dining room and Eliana's blonde hair stirred gently from the draft.

"Hello, Eliana." Jude's eyes fell on the little girl. "Can I come in?"

"I suppose so, she said," sounding unsure.

"Who's there? Judas, is that you?" Beth stepped from a back room, cradling a double-barrel shotgun in her arms.

"Whoa, it's just me, Jude; I'm unarmed," Jude joked nervously.

"Where's Eric?" Beth asked.

"He's not here, it's just me. I've been thinking about what you said the other day, and I had a couple more questions."

"What sort of questions?" Beth asked, glancing at Eliana.

Jude noticed the shotgun shift slightly toward him. "Uh, are you gonna shoot me?"

"Hold out your right wrist so I can see it," Beth said.

"My wrist?" Jude pulled his sleeves above both wrists and twisted them for her to examine. "Why do you want to—?"

"And your phone," she interjected. "Let me see your phone."

Jude slid his Droid from its case and placed it on the floor. "Ms. LeHan, are you planning on shooting me?" His voice shook a little this time.

Beth paused a moment. "Just come in and shut the door."

Jude pushed the door against the wind as Beth shuffled Eliana out of the room.

"Now, what questions?" Beth asked, as Jude turned to face her.

Jude cleared his throat nervously; she still held the shotgun.

39

Eric pulled his motorcycle up to a metal gate. "The note didn't say anything about a gate," he said to Mag, killing the motor. The padlock held a chain below a faded orange NO TRESPASSING sign.

Dense briers were shadowed by a mixed grove of leafless oak and maple trees. The tangle of limbs twisted to form an impenetrable fence. A narrow path snaked slightly downhill through grey trees, disappearing around a bend ahead.

"I don't think I can maneuver the bike through the weeds," Eric said. "You up for a walk?"

"Guess we don't have a choice," Mag slid off the motorcycle and stretched her legs.

Eric knew allowing her to come was a bad idea. Even though she had been adamant about coming, putting her safety in jeopardy was reckless of him. Maybe he was feeling the guilt of allowing himself a brief moment in her arms. Or maybe it was just fatigue followed by bad judgment. Whatever his reason, it was too late now. He didn't have time to take her back.

Eric rubbed his arm as he sized up the gate. "I'll get over and give you a hand up," he said.

"Don't worry about me," Mag smiled. "I can manage."

Eric leaned his bike against the gate and slipped his handgun into his back pocket. With a fluid motion, he scaled the gate. Mag pulled herself over, pausing to smile at Eric, who was offering her his hand. She accepted the help and continued to hold his hand as they walked together under the canopy of bare tree limbs.

The path was barely more than two worn tire tracks, separated by brittle tufts of dead grass and wilted ivy. A frigid wind whistled through the trees as the sun began its slow arc to the west. "I'm not sure what to expect here," Eric confessed, pulling his woven cap over his ears. "The note's pretty cryptic, not a lot of information." He adjusted the handgun and glanced at Mag. He could feel that she was trembling. He pulled her close. "You're freezing," he said.

"No, I'm fine," she whispered, watching a thicket of willows sway as she walked past.

Ahead, the path widened, opening to an overgrown field of dried fescue. It descended sharply to a ravine with a small stream edged by scattered oaks. Across the stream, the landscape jutted upward, becoming a limestone hill choked in underbrush and pine trees. Nestled on top of the hill, barely visible through the pines, was the shell of an old homestead.

At the base of the hill, stood a pair of wooden doors. "A cave entrance or a mine," he decided, touching the rough lumber.

"Maybe we shouldn't go any further." Mag's voice was barely audible.

Eric rubbed his injured arm, the familiar twinge of uneasiness grew. He glanced at his watch. "It's getting late, and we certainly don't want to be stuck here in the cold." He turned his attention to Mag. "Just stay here. I don't know what I'm walking into, and I couldn't forgive myself if something were to happen to you. Let me check it out—I'll be right back."

"You're not leaving me out here alone," Mag stated flatly. "We both go in, or we both go home."

"Mag, please," Eric said, exhaling a deep breath.

"I can take care of myself, Eric. I want to help you."

Eric glanced at the sky, calculating the fading light. "Okay," he whispered, "but stay close to me."

The cellar doors stood nine feet tall and were constructed of weathered oak. Six hinges outlined the doors, connecting them to the rocky sides of the natural cave opening. Two circular handles hung chest high. Eric slid the .380 from his back pocket and pulled the iron ring of the nearest door. The rusty hinges protested as the door popped and cracked open. A damp smell of decayed leaves and mold issued from the crack. Eric planted his feet and pulled harder. The door squealed and swung wide, pounding against the limestone hillside. They stood together, staring into the dark cavity.

"I forgot to bring a flashlight," Eric said, as a matter of fact.

"All I have is a lighter," Mag offered, digging it out of her pocket.

Eric checked the sky again, cursing his lack of preparation. "It'll have to do." He led the way into the mouth of the cave with the flickering light. A few yards inside, the walls expanded outward and the ceiling disappeared into darkness. An underground stream ran down the middle of the cavern, making the ground soggy.

Another hundred yards found them standing in complete darkness. The entryway was out of sight, and the plastic lighter had become hot in Eric's hand. He extinguished the flame, allowing it to cool down. "This is ridiculous," Eric whispered. "How could Gwen be in a place like this?" He took a deep breath and shook his head. "Jude was right, this is a really bad idea. Coming here without a plan, without backup, without even a flashlight..." *and you're endangering the life of a woman you barely know,* he thought.

Eric felt a coldness stir around his feet. Mag had said nothing since entering the cave. Fear began to gnaw at the back of his neck and spine.

He swore under his breath, rubbing his arm. "Maybe we should go back and get some help." Eric reached for Mag, but she wasn't there.

"Who are you?" The voices were sharp, like a hiss. They seemed to assault him from every direction.

"Mag?" Eric fumbled the warm lighter, dropping his handgun.

"Mag!" Eric clicked the lighter frantically. The sparks illuminated the blackness for split seconds at a time. He caught a glimpse of her, standing in front of him.

Her eyes were wide and black as coal.

The lighter ignited, briefly illuminating something in her hand. Mag held a metal stake above her head. The voices that came from her throat were not her own.

"Your soul belongs to us now!" they screeched, lunging at Eric.

Eric swung the lighter wildly, igniting his sleeve. The voices screeched as the stake swung down, burying into Eric's leg, just above his right knee.

He twisted in pain, pulling his leg away. Swinging his burning sleeve at Mag, he stumbled backward, dragging his throbbing leg behind him. She jerked away from the fire, giving Eric the opportunity to clamber back the way they had come. The smoke stung his eyes, blurring his bearings and causing his feet to tangle. He dropped into a smoldering heap in the mud.

Pushing himself up, he groped ahead, eyes wide but unable to see. He searched the darkness over his shoulder. Not far behind, a pair of yellow eyes followed, bouncing in a rhythmic jog.

His injured leg had become a dead weight, slowing his escape.

"God, help me!" he begged through clenched teeth. His leg buckled, dropping him to the mud again. He could hear his heart pounding in his ears as a warm stream of blood gushed from his leg. Staggering ahead, he followed the wall with one hand, holding the other in front of his face.

"God, please help me," he pleaded again. "Get me out of here."

A gust of wind carried the scent of pine; he was close to the entrance. The breeze rejuvenated his determination, giving him the strength to plod forward and keep his blurred mind conscious.

He glanced behind again, but saw nothing but darkness. Mag was not there.

Using the breeze as a guide, he staggered a few yards before toppling over the threshold of the cave. He collapsed into the haven of tall fescue as the wooden doors slammed shut behind him.

Cellar Doors

40

Jude slid around the winding chert road with a cyclone of fallen leaves billowing behind. Rounding the curve, he saw the gate with Eric's motorcycle leaning against it. He aimed the truck at the padlock and thundered through the gate with a paint-stripping squeal.

A crop of saplings parted, opening to the field of fescue and the limestone hillside beyond. With the ravine in view, Jude stomped the brake pedal, sliding sideways across the lower portion of the field. The engine stuttered before dying as he kicked the door open and sprinted down the hill. Eric's body was near the entrance. He was moving slowly, obviously hurt and disoriented, but alive.

Jude knelt next to Eric, his leg was caked with blood and mud; crimson bubbled through his fingers, dripping on the dirt beneath him. It stained the ground in dark patches. Seeing Jude, he winced and tried to push himself up. His right coat sleeve was charred; pink flesh exposed and burned. He was trembling.

"You're going to be okay, Eric. Just take it easy a minute."

Eric propped himself with his good arm. "I don't know what went wrong in there. I was trying to find Gwen... but it was so dark." He squeezed his eyes shut. "I should have listened to you, Jude. I should have waited."

"You're in shock," Jude said, pulling off his jacket.

"And I didn't find Gwen. I don't even know if she's in there." Eric gripped Jude's shirt. "I didn't find her, Jude."

"It's alright, Eric. I spoke with the sheriff. He'll be here in a few minutes."

"It's Mag. She attacked me. Something's wrong with her." Eric exhaled a sharp breath and tried to stand. "I can't let you go alone; she's still in there." The tear in his leg opened wider, exposing meat and tissue. Blood drained from his face as he slumped back to the ground.

Jude wrapped his jacket around Eric's leg in a makeshift tourniquet before standing and facing the doors.

"Beth thinks you're involved in this somehow." Eric locked eyes with Jude. "Tell me it's not true."

"I love your sister, Eric. And if she's in there, I'll find her. I think I'm a little better equipped now that I understand what we're up against."

"You can't go in there alone."

"I'm not alone anymore, Eric."

A breath of musty air issued from the cave as Jude stepped in. Darkness seeped around the edges, swirling in the fading light. A mournful sigh echoed from somewhere deep within the cavity.

With each step, his indignation grew. He wasn't intimidated by doubt this time. It was different; he was different. Something new coursed through his veins. An electrical current crackling just below the surface of his consciousness. His stride was purposeful, almost jogging through the inky blackness. His conversation with Beth had been pivotal for him. She had stirred questions that had festered in the deepest recesses of his soul for most of his life. Questions about his existence, his purpose. His worth. He had grown to believe we were alone in the universe. Just specks of dust spinning through space. It was a lonely philosophy, but he had never been presented with any proof to cause him to question the idea. Nor had he considered the possibility of a spiritual realm existing in step with ours. Until now.

He fished a small penlight from his front pocket. The sliver of light sliced the darkness like a silver beacon; bouncing around the cavern, fighting against the sea of shifting blackness that threatened to swallow it. He was now faced with the fact that a spiritual realm did indeed exist. And with that revelation came a very important, and for him, life altering question: Was someone or something in charge of this realm? Was there a hierarchy or ultimate authority? Was there true order in the universe? Was there a God?

The cave was filled with more than just simple darkness. The blackness moved with calculated purpose. Swirling, probing, searching for weakness. A presence lurked just out of reach of his tiny beacon; something foreign and unnatural. Something evil. His voice thundered off the damp walls.

"Gwen!" The echo was stifled.

A throaty chuckle to his right. Something passed beneath him, around his feet. A clammy draft ran like fingers up his leg and across his back. Jude guided his light around the cave. Pockets of quartz blinked back at him and mud caked to his boots, weighing down his stride.

Jude was introduced to the answer at Beth's house. And it didn't come through a philosophical debate. It was more of a revelation. A simple truth that transcended the scientific arguments that had shaped his world view. He was introduced to God. And as it turned out, God had been expecting him.

A chiseled door stood outlined in a yellow light ahead. Jude didn't hesitate as he approached. Holding his breath, he kicked the door open with a bone-jarring thud. Yellow candlelight tumbled from the room, chasing the shadows into corners. Jude stepped in. A lone, wooden table held a silver platter with burning candles. A burgundy rug stretched across the damp floor, covering most of the small room. The ceiling was lost in darkness, extending somewhere beyond the candle's reach. A second door stood secure against the far wall; a metal clasp held it tight.

"Gwen, are you here?" Jude spoke softly, approaching the door.

Something stirred on the other side.

Jude placed his hand on the doorknob, turning it with a rusty moan. It was locked.

A cold sensation settled on the back of Jude's neck as the pressure in the room changed, becoming heavy. But rather than fear, Jude felt a surge of lightning race through his body; the muscles in his jaw tensed. He turned, facing the door.

A woman draped in a black robe stood motionless in the doorway. Her face was powder white, lips pale. But her eyes were as black as the cave she had come from. Jude recognized the woman; the nurse from the hospital. Mag.

She spoke, but her words were distorted, guttural. Not her own. *"We have killed. We have stolen, and we will destroy you."* She grinned at Jude, her black eyes twitching in their sockets.

Jude turned his attention back to the door. Grabbing the knob with both hands, he leaned his shoulder against the wood and pushed. "Gwen, stand away from the door." It groaned under the pressure but refused to open. Dark oppression flickered the candles.

Jude held his breath and slammed his shoulder into the center of the door. A garbled language issued from Mag's throat. The chant became louder as the dank air in the room began to move. Jude dug his feet into the rug and slammed the door for the third time. The door split, bowing to Jude's will.

"Gwen?" Jude questioned the darkness that met him. The room stirred and a form dragged itself toward the light. He reached for Gwen, pulling her out of the mud to his chest. Other than the clean streaks from her tears, her face was dirty and peppered with dried blood.

"I knew you would come," she said, shivering.

Her fingers were bloodied from scratching at the door, and her hair and clothes were matted and stained. "It's okay now," he whispered, helping her to her feet. "Just stay near me."

The candlelight flickered violently in the stale air, tormented by unseen forces. Casting erratic shadows on the limestone walls, the flames shivered and jerked, mixing the shadows with dark blotches that circled and crawled around the edges of the room. Mag stood in the mouth of the doorway, blocking the only way out; a twisted grin stretched across her face. Dark eyes darted from Jude to Gwen, waiting for them.

"There are more here," Gwen whispered to Jude, her eyes wide with fear. "I heard them crying; they sounded like children. There must be other cells."

Mag moved closer to them, her shoulders hunched forward as if she carried a heavy weight. *"We will devour your souls—"* A hand disappeared into the folds of her robe, producing a railroad spike.

Gwen could feel Jude's heartbeat drumming in a slow, solid rhythm in her hand. He didn't seem panicked or afraid. Taking a deep breath, he stepped toward Mag. "Gwen, stay beside me." Jude locked eyes with Mag. "And you," he pointed his finger at her as he stepped closer, "get behind me!"

"You have no authority here," Mag spat, taking a step backward. *"You will rot in this den of iniquity forever!"* But there was a quiver of doubt in the voices.

"You're wrong," Jude spoke softly this time. "It is you who are powerless here."

Mag screeched and lunged at Jude. The stake flashed in the candlelight as Jude twisted, grabbing her wrists. She glared at Jude, *"She is ours! You will not take her!"* A multitude of voices spewed from her mouth, none of them her own. He struggled against the strength of multiple spirits. "Leave her alone!" Jude commanded the darkness within her, looking beyond the dark pupils. "Let her go!"

Mag convulsed, as though struck in the gut.

She pulled against Jude's grip in desperation. Her lips parted, revealing a set of yellow eyes backing away deep into her throat. She convulsed again, spraying black bile down the front of her robe. The candles flickered and blew out, plunging the room into complete darkness. The metal stake clattered against the wall.

"Noooo!" Dark voices shrieked in unison from around the room.

The screams were followed by a flapping sound that echoed off the walls, trailing up toward the high ceiling into silence. Mag fell limp, breaking Jude's grip on her wrists.

Jude retrieved his penlight. The feeble light found Gwen, sitting against the wall near the doorway, her knees folded tightly against her chest. Fresh tears ran down her face. Mag lay face down at Jude's feet, her body quivering slightly. Jude touched her shoulder, and she stirred, slowly scooting her legs under and pushing herself to her knees. Her red hair was damp and disheveled, shrouding her face. Jude lifted her chin to meet his eyes. Violet eyes blinked from behind her hair.

"Are you okay?" Jude asked, pushing the hair from her face.

"I think so." Her voice was small and brittle, but feminine. "Please take me out of here." There was fear and confusion in her eyes.

Gwen appeared next to Jude and helped Mag to her feet. They flanked her on either side like human crutches and shuffled through the doorway into the open cave.

41

E ric propped himself on elbows as Jude, Gwen and Mag appeared at the cave's entrance.

"Gwen!" Eric forced himself to his knees as Gwen fell into his arms.

"Eric, you're hurt!" Gwen sobbed.

"I'm fine." Eric blinked back tears and locked his gaze on Mag. He was about to say something, but instead settled back to the ground, feeling dizzy.

Jude helped Mag to the grass. She was disoriented, staring at the dried blood on her fingers.

"It's okay, Eric." Jude noticed his stare. "Mag needs our help, too."

A siren squawked twice as the sheriff's patrol car swung around a grove of pines and came into view. An ambulance followed the sheriff while JD's patrol car pulled in front of the cave's entrance. The sheriff emerged from his car and exchanged words with the EMT. JD drew his firearm and disappeared into the cave.

Eric was still watching Mag. "She tried to kill me, Jude. She doesn't need our help—she needs jail time."

"Trust me, Eric. I'll explain everything."

Jude stood to meet JD, who exited the cave and was jogging toward the group.

"Is everyone okay?" The deputy searched each face, stopping at Mag's. A paramedic knelt next to Eric to assess his injuries. A second EMT brought a stretcher.

"What happened here?" JD turned to Jude.

"There are children in the cave." Jude nodded in the direction of the cavern. "We need to get back in there and find them."

JD followed his gaze to the doors. "Children? Did you see children?"

"No, but Gwen heard crying." Jude looked to Gwen for confirmation.

She was huddled next to Eric, holding his hand in hers. Shivering. A look of horror masked her face. She didn't take her eyes off JD.

"Gwen?" Jude asked.

JD smiled at Gwen, resting his hand on the butt of his revolver. "I didn't see any children in there. Obviously, she's in shock," he said. "The ambulance can only take one at a time, so you three will ride with me to the hospital, and I'll see that she's taken care of," JD stepped closer.

The sheriff hobbled across the uneven ground, nursing his hip with a slight grimace. "JD, go see what's in that house on top of the hill. I've notified SWAT. It'll take them a couple hours to mobilize and get here from the city. Meanwhile, I want the perimeter cleared and sealed."

JD's smile faded. "Sheriff, we can check this out ourselves. I don't see any reason to involve a SWAT team."

"JD, go check out that shack, and let me do the thinking."

JD glanced at Gwen before turning his attention to the hillside. "Okay, Sheriff," he said coolly. "I'll check out the house."

Gwen kept her eyes locked on JD until he disappeared into the low limbs and thicket.

"It's okay, Gwen," Jude assured her. "You're safe now."

With the deputy out of sight, Gwen pulled Jude close. "Don't trust them," her voice shook with fear.

Jude pulled away, confused. "Don't trust who?"

Gwen motioned to the patrol car. "Don't trust any of them."

The paramedics helped Eric into the back of the ambulance. The flashing lights alternated red and white as it pulled away.

"Sheriff, I think we need another ambulance here." Jude motioned to his truck. "I don't think my truck can make the trip to the hospital."

"It's already on the way, son," the sheriff said. "I called a second one in when we pulled up. Should be here any minute."

As if on cue, a boxy, white ambulance pitched and careened over the uneven ground toward them.

"I'll get us out of here," he whispered to Gwen.

Cellar Doors

42

Gerri Coe was conscious to the throbbing of her heart in her ears. Her eyes were sore and swollen shut. Despite the cold, beads of sweat trickled down her face, irritating a laceration on her cheek.

She rolled her head back and forced her eyes open, taking a moment to adjust to the dim light. Her arms and legs were bound behind her back with a rubber bungee cord, and her hands and fingertips ached from the constriction. Wide duct tape coiled around her head and across her mouth, pulling at her hair like sticky hands.

She sat in the middle of a vacant room, facing a closed door. Floral wallpaper draped the room; its tired edges curled and worn from years of neglect. To her right, a solitary window fought to hold back the knot of gnarled limbs that swayed and scratched with every cough of wind. Memories began to filter back.

"ID and registration, please." She recalled the blue lights flashing in the rear-view mirror.

"I didn't think I was speeding, Officer," Gerri said, *rummaging through the glove box.*

"No ma'am. You have a tail light out."

"Oh, I didn't know," she said.

The officer took the identification from her. "Could you please step out of the car, ma'am?"

"Out of the car? But…"

"Please, ma'am. I need you to see the tail light."

"Officer, I believe you," she said. "I'll get it fixed as soon as I get back to town."

"Yes, ma'am, but I still need you to exit the vehicle; it's procedure. I just need you to verify the light is out."

Gerri clicked her seatbelt and opened the door. "I've never heard of a procedure like that," she said.

The officer slid his MagLite from his belt loop and followed her to the back of the car...

Gerri dropped her head and swallowed the panic. The empty room spun in sync with her churning stomach.

And now, she was here in what looked like the bedroom of an abandoned house. She glanced out the window at the setting sun. Her cramping legs told her it had been hours, maybe days, since they had been straightened.

Judas slipped a key ring from his pocket, and unlocked the padlock securing the chain to the front door of the shack. He squinted at the dusk sky before cracking the door and sliding inside. Dim sunlight fought to break through decades of tree sap that caked the windowpanes. He walked past each empty room to the rear of the house.

Thumbing through the keys, he jabbed one into the padlock that was clasped to a bedroom door. It opened to a small room with a wooden chair bolted to the floor. Gerri pulled and squirmed against the cords that bound her to the chair. The tight bungees had turned her hands and fingers an angry purple.

He stepped in front of her, drew the revolver and clicked the hammer back. Gerri squeezed her eyes shut, the duct tape muffling a whimper. She felt the cool metal of the barrel press against her temple.

He chuckled.

"So, you're awake," he licked his lips, tasting her fear. "I hope the accommodations have been adequate."

Gerri flexed her jaws, pulling against the tape.

"I guess you're wondering why you're here. Or if I'm going to kill you." His voice grew dark. "Is that what plagues you, old woman? You wonder if I have the stomach to pull the trigger?"

Gerri wrestled with her constraints; fresh tears dropped from her chin.

"Well," he whispered through clenched teeth. "Your mortality hangs on the next thirty seconds."

He relaxed his grip on the pistol and smiled.

"I have a couple questions concerning our friends."

Cellar Doors

43

Gwen and Mag were secure in the second ambulance when JD emerged from the tree-line. "What'd you find up there?" the sheriff asked.

"Just an old shack. It's empty." JD watched Jude squeeze in next to Gwen. A paramedic shut the rear doors, and the ambulance pulled away. He watched the truck round the corner. "Your perimeter's clear, Sheriff. I'll follow them in; get their statements."

Sheriff Roy waited until the ambulance and JD's squad car were out of sight. He glanced up the hill in the direction of the shack. Something wasn't adding up. Two decades in law enforcement had been rough on his body, but had sharpened his mind.

The devil's always in the details.

Roy sized up the hill and rubbed his sore hip. "This is gonna hurt."

He started up the bluff, fighting for each foothold. Grunting past roots and slippery leaves, his fingers fumbled from sapling to sapling. He recalled the look on JD's face when he came down from investigating the shack. *He was flustered. Flustered and agitated.*

He pushed ahead, reaching for a limb. His foot twisted and dropped into a hidden sinkhole. Wincing, he pitched forward, grappling with a nest of willow shoots before crumpling to his knees. A bevy of loose rocks scattered down the hill with leaf-covered snowballs. The pain in his hip rallied and shot down his leg as he rolled to his knees, waiting for the throbbing to subside.

He peered ahead. Through the brambles and low limbs, he could make out the sagging roofline of the abandoned house. He checked his watch. The sun would drop behind the hills soon, and the night promised to be cold.

He found his feet and carefully settled weight on the twisted ankle, trying to ignore the fresh pain by focusing on details. Jude mentioned some threatening phone calls both he and Gwen had gotten before her abduction. And there had been a missing persons report filed on her Aunt Gerri. *A report I never saw,* he thought.

There was another detail. When JD returned from investigating the shack, his holster guard was not snapped. A small observation. It could have been pulled loose by weeds or brush. But JD, like any officer, grows accustomed to habitually checking his equipment—constantly checking snaps and zippers was an occupational habit.

The sheriff could now see the front porch and the weathered shutters nailed closed. A rusty chain snaked through the front door with a bleached NO TRESPASSING sign that warned prosecution. Whether JD's pistol guard was accidentally unsnapped or he drew his firearm, the circumstances didn't matter. Something had JD preoccupied enough to neglect his firearm.

The sheriff paused on the porch to study the lock. Fresh scratches marred the perimeter of the keyhole. It had been opened recently.

He slid the MagLite from his belt and broke rectangles of glass from the nearest window. He shined the flashlight into the opening and wiped irritating sweat from his eyes. Crunching glass under his boot, he heaved himself over the sill and wormed into the front room.

The flashlight illuminated a dismal scene. Dead vines wandered up the walls and the smell of mold and vermin seeped from the rafters. A corner of the ceiling had collapsed, allowing leaves and broken limbs to blow in. The sheriff shuffled through the rotting drift, following the beam of light around an archway to a closed bedroom door. He rattled the doorknob and focused his MagLite on the padlock.

A muffled noise responded from the other side. His heartbeat quickened and that sick feeling stirred his stomach again. He settled his weight against the door and pushed.

Solid.

He fished his Leatherman out and went to work on the screws holding the clasp.

Cellar Doors

44

Ink & Baud Building

A Bach CD looped softly from hidden speakers near the bookshelf in the corner. The lights were dim, giving the room a sophisticated, yet comfortable ambience. This evening, four high-backed chairs surrounded the mahogany table. A fifth chair sprawled on the floor; a sixth leaned against the bookshelf.

A woman sat in the chair, her head pinched awkwardly against her shoulder. Her glazed eyes stared at the ceiling through horn-rimmed glasses. A single crimson streak trickled from her chestnut hairline and pooled in the corner of her left eye. It overflowed and drained into her mouth. At her feet, a lime-flavored Perrier lay on its side, chugging quietly into the carpet.

A second body was crumpled in the shadow of the table; a man in a charcoal suit. A dark stain crept across his back, soaking the plush carpet beneath. Judas sat at the head of the table, thumbing through a manila folder while mechanically spinning a handgun on the high gloss tabletop. He didn't seem concerned that the gun was scratching the deep polish.

He whistled under his breath. "Excellent penmanship." He smiled at the dead man on the floor. "But I have to confess, I'm a little surprised you'd choose to keep such sensitive information in a fifty-cent school folder. What's the matter, don't trust your fancy technology?"

Bach's hypnotic piano solo drifted around the room.

"But," he glanced at the gun thoughtfully, "you had the foresight to soundproof the room. Well, I must applaud your sense of intuition. Talk about thinking ahead."

Judas stood and peeled latex gloves from his hands. He paused a moment to relish his handiwork. The splatter marks on the walls looked like a wet dog had shaken itself dry. Dark splotches trailed like thick molasses down the side of the bookshelf. Pools of blood began to coagulate on the tabletop.

"What a mess," he chuckled, stuffing the gloves into his pocket.

Finding the High Echelon had been more difficult than expected. He remembered his first attempt. The reverse cell phone trace bounced off numerous repeaters before fizzling in a small village in Malaysia. He wasn't too upset with that failure; he knew it was a long shot. The Group was good at hiding; they wouldn't be found easily.

Next, he focused on trying to uncover the business front they were using to hide their operation. He spent late nights and long hours tracking down every snitch and street contact he had in the city. The lowlife either didn't know what the High Echelon was or knew enough to keep their mouths shut.

Undaunted, he pulled hundreds of business licenses at the county courthouse, hoping to find something that looked shady. But nothing caught his attention.

They could be anywhere, posing as anything. Flower shop, liquor store. Church. As far as he knew, they were hiding in the back room of a children's clothing store.

He was running short on ideas when they made a mistake. Judas replayed the event in his head. His contact had called, spouting off about losing her seat on the Hierarchy, or whatever. She was frantic; no doubt being pressured from the Group to come up with some answers. Calling or texting to threaten him had become her new past-time. Judas smiled at the woman in the chair. Until this evening, he had never met her. But he still knew things about her. He had been piecing her profile puzzle together for awhile now. He knew she was a middle-aged, educated woman. Knew that she was either a lawyer or a psychiatrist. Knew she was very careful and articulate. Of course, her contact number was always scrambled.

Except for her last call.

"What happened, did the stress finally get to you?" Judas whispered to the corpse, remembering her one and only mistake. "Did you even realize what you had done? I mean, did you get a weird sinking feeling in your gut when you realized you'd dialed my number from your unsecured home phone?"

Judas flashed his teeth at the woman. "You had to know I'd come." He rubbed his bristly chin and watched her. "Maybe you wanted me to come. That's it, isn't it? You were tired of the game, tired of the hunt. Just wanted to take the easy way out. Maybe you knew your days were numbered, too."

Judas licked his lips and basked in the memory. A simple *69 revealed her phone number. A couple hours staking her residence and following her around town paid off when she drove to the backside of the Industrial Park.

"You let the pressure get to you, didn't you?" Judas cleared his throat and lowered his voice. "Listen, I know you said some pretty hateful things to me. Just want you to know, I don't hold them against you." He stared at the dead woman as if listening to her response. "You're welcome." He hesitated. "Oh, the music? Very soothing, don't you think?"

He leaned back in his chair and closed his eyes. "I believe this piece is a selection from the *Well-Tempered Clavier*." He paused, waiting for the corpse to be impressed. "Oh please, now you're just trying to flatter me. I'm not that cultured. I peeked at the CD case."

He caressed the folder on the table. It contained detailed information on the Chapter's clientele, as well as the names and addresses of the Recruiters, Taskmasters, and the identities of the Six Seat Hierarchy. But next to the folder was the real prize, the reason he found it necessary to make his uninvited house call; the payoff of months of planning. All for a phone. "Well, it's not really just a phone, now is it?" He nudged the dead man with his foot. "Oh, aren't you a sly one," he whispered. "I guess you love technology after all."

On the smart phone's screen, a colored map displayed a handful of blinking numbers. Each number represented an embedded tracking chip. "Every living member in the Chapter is accounted for now." He nodded to the woman. "Oh, and some dead ones."

Judas focused on the folder. "So, let's play a game, shall we?" He glanced around the room and cleared his throat before selecting a sheet of paper. "Let's guess which number belongs to which name." He found the three numbers in closest proximity. "First, we have my esteemed colleague, Dr. Gail Morrah. Psychiatrist, age thirty-eight. Psychiatrist! I knew it." He nodded triumphantly at his former contact.

"Uh, next we have a Dr. Vic Kenan. Is there a Dr. Kenan in the house?" Judas waited for a response. "Well, that must be our friend on the floor, then." He chuckled and winked at the dead woman. "I'm afraid he's dead." Judas emphasized his statement by nudging the dead man again.

He looked back at the list. "Oh, what have we here? Looks like we forgot to scratch Reverend Ferrell C's name from roll call. I believe we're all aware of the unfortunate chain of events that led to his untimely passing." Judas snickered at the thought. "All I want to know is, whose idea was it to put me in charge of burying that necklace in his stomach? I mean, Dr. Kenan, according to your file, you're the surgeon in the group."

Judas' smile faded quickly as his attention snapped to the dead man on the floor. "Because I'm not medically trained," he said, answering a question that was never asked.

His mood turned dark and solemn.

"Because if you wanted a nice, pretty suture, you should have done it yourself." Judas ground the words with dark sarcasm and dropped his eyes to the gun on the table. The sides of his neck began to flush. He was about to say something when his train of thought was broken.

"What did you say?" He focused on the woman's unblinking eyes and smiled. "I see. You're probably right."

He regarded Kenan with contempt. "Is that true, Kenan? My friend says you didn't have the guts to do it yourself." Judas laughed as if suddenly catching the punch line. "Guts! Oh, I get it." He looked admirably at the woman. "Oh, Dr. Morrah, you have such a way with words." His gaze settled on the dead man. "So what about it, Doctor. Afraid to get that nice suit grimy?"

He tilted his head back and laughed with the corpses.

Judas turned his attention to the handgun on the table: Eric's .380. Complete with his oily fingerprints on the safety and barrel. Judas smiled at his own resourcefulness. "As you well know, I do my best work by virtue of other's incompetence." He paused for effect with a hateful grin. "I found the gun he left in the shaft." He now addressed the dead man. "So now, when you are found, there will be no question who left you here."

He took a rectangular box from his jacket pocket and placed it on the table. It held two sections of glass. Each section was smudged with a fingerprint and protected by clear Saran Wrap. Prints lifted from Eric's home. Judas removed the first section of wrap and pressed it against the tabletop near the folder. He lifted it away, leaving the unmistakable outline of a fingerprint. He planted the second on the entryway doorknob.

He wasn't as worried about local forensics finding the prints as he was about the High Echelon's people finding them.

"Oh yes, they'll investigate, too," he explained to the woman. "They'll have people crawling all over this place." He smiled. "They'll demand answers. They'll want to know how their state-of-the-art security was breached; wanting to find the genius who somehow outsmarted them."

Judas straightened to admire his work on the doorknob. "Oh, you're right," he said over his shoulder. "Heads will definitely roll." He retrieved the rectangular box and dropped it in his pocket. "I think it would be fitting for our gunslinging friend to take credit for this one."

He picked up the folder and the transponder and hesitated, as if trying to find the right words. "Okay, I've got to get to the hospital and take care of a couple things. And I have a favor to ask." Judas held up his hands and grinned at the woman. "I know, I know, we've technically only just met, but I feel we have a common rapport. You know, a mutual struggle. I just need you to keep our little rendezvous tonight a secret."

He shook his head as he listened for the woman's response. "Well, I appreciate your loyalty, and share your concern." His smile faded. "Honestly, I don't trust our Dr. Kenan here either. I mean, a man who can't do his own dirty work is not a man to be trusted." Disdain dripped from his words as he considered the dead man.

"Oh my, Dr. Morrah, I do like the way you think."

Moments later, Judas quietly left the boardroom. The entryway door softly clicked shut in his wake, and the room grew still. Bach continued his haunted composition; the dead playing for the dead.

The bright streak running down the woman's face had become a thin, dark line against her drained features. The man on the floor was now lying on his back. His ivory teeth glistened with a fresh, jagged smile.

His lips and tongue had been removed.

45

Beth LeHan had spent the day packing her life into cardboard boxes. Tomorrow she would take Eliana and disappear again. She was thinking Texas. Maybe Montana. Somewhere open and vast. Somewhere Eliana could run and play without fear of being discovered.

They'd find a small home with lots of land and maybe a pond. Eliana would like feeding the fish; maybe they'd get a dog. And find a good church. Beth leaned back in her rocking chair. Their plans would have to wait until tomorrow. Tonight, she was exhausted. Time to relax and rest her bones.

She silently rocked and sipped her hot tea. It felt good on her stomach, which had been acting up lately. Her Bible lay open to a verse in Jeremiah. She smiled as she read the promise: *"For I know the plans I have for you, declares the Lord, plans to prosper you and not to harm you, plans to give you hope and a future..."*

She watched the flames dance in the fireplace. She found comfort in this promise, especially the part about having hope and a future.

She closed the Bible and reflected. She still struggled with trust. For a long time, she had been forced to suspect everything and everyone. Her life had literally depended on her ability to deceive and manipulate others. Now that she was free, she was slowly learning to die to her old nature. Every day was a challenge to trust herself less and her new Lord more. She understood that perfect love would cast out fear, and one of the fruits of true love was trust. But lately, her suspicious nature was trying to creep back. She was having trouble distinguishing between simple mistrust and discernment.

Her mind wandered to Gwen and Eric. They were clueless of the powers at work around them. Oblivious to the dangers that lurked in the shadows.

She considered Jude. Initially, she had an odd feeling about him. But she had been wrong. He had come to her with concerns about phone calls he and Gwen had gotten. Threatening voices mixed in static. He feared the Group was responsible and hoped she could help. But more importantly, he had questions about her faith.

Her mind wandered to her past life. She remembered the foreboding and dark excitement she felt when her contact, Judas, paged her with a job to fill. The hateful sense of satisfaction she felt as she destroyed a life. The shame and guilt that always followed. Beth closed her eyes and rebuked the cloud that had settled over her.

"That's not me anymore," she said out loud. "I am no longer bound by that life, or that condemnation."

The forgiveness and assurance was always there, and she basked in the welcome warmth. But she sensed something else. Tangled in the forgiveness and assurance was a gentle tug; a persistent whisper. She tried to bury the soft voice with logical arguments and simple rationale, but it always resurfaced.

Trust Me, the voice would echo.

But it was just too hard. There was one thing she just couldn't give up. One last hold she hadn't learned to pry from her will. And it broke her heart to think about it.

After a few moments, she opened her eyes and was aware of her surroundings. The grandfather clock chimed gently from the corner. The house was dark and still. The floor lamp next to her rocking chair blinked once and dimmed.

There was something else.

Something old and familiar.

Something evil.

"Jesus. Jesus. Jesus. Jesus."

Beth stopped rocking and whispered the name over and over. She rose from the chair and set the Bible on the cushion. For a moment, she stood quietly and just listened. From the back bedroom, she heard the soft rustle of Eliana shifting in her bed. She could make out the wind pushing against a loose windowpane in the dining room. She could hear the gurgling of water.

"Jesus. Jesus. Jesus," she repeated as she stepped out of the living room into the small dining room that joined the kitchen.

Beth stepped around the corner and felt her toes nudge the threshold of linoleum separating the dining room hardwood. A dim light over the sink spotlighted a running faucet. Beth turned the knob off and paused at the sink. She hadn't left the water running.

A faint creaking of floor slats caught her attention; it came from the back of the house. Sometimes the old house would shift and settle, causing the floors and rafters to complain against rusty nails. Sometimes the freezing wind would expand the metal pipes. The sound came again. This time from the bedrooms, like the shifting of weight. Beth imagined a faceless Judas hunched in a dark corner, waiting to steal away with Eliana.

She hurried to her room.

The floor squeaked beneath her feet as she clipped down the short hallway ending at two closed bedroom doors. She twisted the knob on Eliana's door and pushed inward. The sweet smells of vanilla and jasmine lingered around the door as she searched the room's corners with her eyes. She listened to the child's quiet breathing for a moment before pulling the door closed again. She turned to face her own bedroom.

She sensed evil in her spirit, but there was no fear. Like a battle-scarred warrior, she felt resolve. Resolve and clarity.

And indignation.

She felt a sudden chill as she pushed open the door.

"Jesus. Jesus. Jesus. Jesus."

A tall shadow eclipsed the window in her room. It crowded the ceiling, its head bent slightly. Yellow saucers glowed without blinking. The smell of old meat caught her breath. For a moment, neither moved.

Then Beth smiled.

"Jesus. Jesus. Jesus." Louder, she chanted the name. "Jesus. Jesus. Jesus." She took a bold step toward the demon. "Jesus. Jesus. Jesus."

A current of adrenaline washed over her, and she took a deep breath and belted out with determined fervor: "Jesus! Jesus! Jesus!"

The yellow eyes tightened to thin slivers.

"Get out of my house!" she commanded. "Get out!" She pointed at the shadow and stepped closer. A low hiss issued from the Implement, and the yellow eyes blinked once before backing into the shadows. Beth took a deep breath and flipped on the overhead light. The room was empty. The silver necklace was wrapped around the foot of her bedpost.

Someone had put the necklace there, which meant she and Eliana had been found for sure. Beth felt a sadness curl around her heart as she unwrapped the necklace from the bedpost. Would it always be this way? Running from place to place, always watching over their shoulders. Always afraid of being found. She walked back to the fireplace and dropped the necklace on the glowing embers. She watched the flames slither around the metal, crackling and spitting as the silver curled on itself like a small snake. The silver ram's horn twisted and blackened. She wished the running would be over by simply destroying the pendant. But she knew it had only just begun. It was time to face facts; she couldn't make Eliana live like this. Not forever.

Trust Me.

Beth stirred the embers and tried to ignore her heart.

46

Sheriff Roy twisted the last screw and clamped the MagLite under his arm. He drew his service revolver.

"Sheriff's Department, I'm coming in." He pushed the door open with the nose of his .38 Smith and Wesson.

The light bobbed around the room, clearing each corner before settling on the wooden chair.

Gerri Coe slumped forward in the chair. Her hands were bound behind her back, swollen fingers dark from blood restriction. The sheriff holstered his revolver and went to work on the restraints. Gerri stirred with a raspy moan; her hands shook slightly as he cut away the cords. She was as cold as ice, and each breath was little more than a shallow wheeze. He traced the side of her neck, finding a weak pulse.

"Can you hear me, Gerri?" Roy's voice bounced around the room and down the dark hallway.

No response.

Her bound ankles were twisted and raw. It was obvious she had been in this same position for some time. Her thin blouse had been no match against the harsh temperature. Pulling off his sports coat, he draped it across her back.

The cold immediately began to permeate past his flannel long-sleeves and undershirt. "We need to get you warm," he said, snapping the police radio from his belt.

He stood the flashlight on the floor as a makeshift lamp and spoke into the radio. "This is Sheriff Roy, copy?" He pressed the talk button and repeated, "This is Sheriff Roy, copy?" In the fuzz, he could hear the faint voice of dispatch.

"Ten-one..." The static grew, engulfing the broken reply.

"Ten-fifty two!" He yelled over the static, "I need an ambulance! Do you copy?" Static mocked the feeble connection and filled the room.

"Blast it all!" Panic crept into the sheriff's voice. He thumbed the mic and waited for a response in the sea of static. He placed the radio next to the flashlight and took a breath. The sheriff shifted weight off his swelling ankle. "Looks like we're on our own."

47

Emergency Physicians Hospital Room 432

"What do you mean *they're gone*? How could they be gone? They've been here less than two hours!" JD's voice shook with irritation.

The emergency room receptionist waited for JD to finish his rant. "I don't know, Deputy, they didn't tell anyone they were leaving; they just left."

"What about the guy with the injured leg?" JD pounded the nurse's desk impatiently.

The nurse fumed at him for a moment before consulting her computer screen. "He's already been stitched up. He's in room 432 for observation until the sedative wears off."

JD pushed away from the desk, bolted past the elevators, and clanged through the metal door leaving the nurse to brood alone. Reaching the 4th floor, he followed the hallway to the room. The bed was disheveled. And empty. JD pushed the heavy bathroom door open; it was empty, too. He jammed the nurse's button with his thumb and waited.

"How may I help you—" a cheery voice began.

"Where is the patient assigned to this room? He should be here, and he's not."

"I'm sorry. Who is this?" The cheer had left her voice.

"I'm a Deputy Sheriff, and I need to speak with the patient who should be in this room!"

"I'm on the way."

JD took a deep breath and settled on the edge of the bed. "It's okay," he spoke to the room. "Everything is under control. Everything is falling into place."

He relaxed and smiled.

And now, there was very little that stood in his way. *A crippled sheriff and a handful of unlucky souls.* "Unlucky souls." His eyes wandered around the room as he verbalized his thought. "My friends have no idea what manner of hell they've stumbled into. My deserved recognition is almost here. Finally, I'll reap what I've sown." JD chuckled quietly. "Reap what I've sown; my, doesn't that sound biblically stuffy."

48

E ric watched JD from the dark room across the hall. Peering through the crack of the open door, he listened to him ramble before the nurse arrived. He waited as JD called dispatch with a cell phone trace. Eric recognized the cell phone number as his own. "You trying to find me, JD?" he whispered. When he was gone, Eric slid the phone from his back pocket. "Well, finding me is not going to be quite that easy."

Eric searched the room finding a box of latex gloves.

He pushed the phone inside a glove, tied a knot in the top, and flushed it down the commode.

"Not sure if it's possible to trace a phone through the city sewer, but maybe it'll buy me a little more time," he mumbled to himself.

Eric steadied himself against the sink and took a personal inventory in the mirror. A bandaged arm from the attack in his living room, a burned forearm, and fresh stitches in his leg from the run-in with Mag. And his head was still spinning from the Vicodin they'd given him.

The last few days had drained the life out of him. And the mix of trauma and painkiller was making it difficult to wrap his head around current events. In the ambulance, Gwen told them it was JD who drugged her. So, until he knew who was honest, trusting the sheriff's department was out.

Beth and Eliana would check into a Motel 6 under a fake name and wait for Eric to contact them when it was safe to leave town for good. Keeping tabs on JD was Eric's idea; didn't want him popping up unexpectedly again. Eric checked the hallway before leaving the room. *But just 'keeping tabs' on the vermin that hurt my sister just doesn't seem... appropriate.*

Eric slid down the stairwell with a more appropriate plan.

49

"**Y**ou're different," Gwen said, watching Jude as he nuzzled the afghan under her chin. She was curled on the loveseat in Mag's living room. The apartment was tucked on the backside of Building C, a two-bedroom with antique white walls and modest furnishings.

Jude handed Gwen a steaming cup. "Why do you say that?"

"In the cave, I was scared. So scared I could barely think. I saw things in there I didn't know existed—things I still can't explain." She paused, remembering. "And the fear I felt was unnatural, stifling. There was a depth of hopelessness that I've never known." Gwen bowed her head as she spoke. "But you, you didn't seem to be affected by any of it. Actually, the things in that room didn't scare you; they were scared *of* you."

Gwen met his eyes. "So, what happened to you, Jude?"

Jude settled next to her and focused on his cup. Cream clouded black coffee. "If I've realized anything over the past few days, it's that there's a whole dimension of life I didn't believe existed. I mean, outside of our mortal cycle of living and dying, there's a deeper reality. There's a reason we're here, Gwen. Life is too brief and fragile to be meaningless." He sipped the coffee. "It took some pretty terrible things to jar me awake to this spiritual realism. I mean, I've been to Sunday school just like everybody else. But honestly, I never really considered church to be that life-altering. Just a religious group therapy, at best." His smiled faded. "But after talking with Beth, I realized there is more to life than just living. Just like there's more to God than just church. She introduced me to the anti-religious Savior who has an orchestrated purpose for us outside of our shallow realities and religious boxes."

"A savior from what?" Mag appeared in the hallway. Her damp hair was swirled around the top of her head and held with a clippie. She had a Band-Aid on her wrist.

Jude considered the question for a moment. "From myself, I think. And from my ideas of who or what I thought God was."

Mag nodded and slid into the overstuffed chair next to the loveseat. Her voice was still weak. "I'd like to believe there's something more out there than what I've seen. My perspective of the world and God is pretty bleak."

"I don't have all the answers, Mag. And I couldn't win a philosophical debate on why I have hope now; I just do."

"I'd like to believe there's a way to untangle the knots I've made of my life." She glanced at Jude. "In the cave, I was aware of what I was doing, but I really couldn't control..." She dropped her eyes to her hands, as tears tumbled down her cheeks.

She glanced at Gwen. "And I'm sorry for what I've put you and Eric through. I'm to blame for so much of it. The attack on Eric at his home was my fault; I gave him the necklace, knowing what would happen. And I seduced him and led him to that cave..." She paused to wipe her eyes. "I led him there to kill him."

Gwen was shivering under the afghan. "But why?" she asked.

"The necklace led us to Eric."

"Us?" There was pain and frustration in Gwen's voice. "You mean you and JD?"

"Yes," Mag said softly. "But I know him as Judas. He was following the necklace to find some people."

"Beth and Eliana?" Jude spoke up.

"No, I mean he was looking for them too, but ultimately he was just using them to find a group of people he and I are a part of."

"The High Echelon?" Jude asked.

Mag was surprised he knew the name. "Yes, the High Echelon," she said. "Judas has some personal vendetta against the Group and has made it his mission to infiltrate it."

"So why us, Mag? Why involve us in his sick nightmare?"

"I really don't know, Gwen. I only know what Judas has told me and what I've been able to piece together. I know he released the demon to find the missing Recruiter and the little girl. And intended to somehow use them to expose the location of the Group's local Chapter."

"That doesn't explain the interest in Eric, or in me."

"I don't think you or Eric were ever supposed to be part of his equation. When Judas was unable to find the woman and the child, he came up with another idea. Maybe he hoped to kidnap you, then use your brother's fury to somehow find the Group."

"But Eric doesn't know where the Group is hiding. He doesn't know anything about any of this."

Mag sat quietly for a moment. "I don't know, Gwen; I really don't know. I'm afraid he may have had more diabolical plans for you."

"You're talking about quotas to fill."

Mag acknowledged her fear with a nod. "Whatever he's planning... I just don't think it's over."

Gwen rose and stood in front of the sliding glass doors. "But what about the children in the cave?" she asked.

Mag's voice was strained. "Gwen, as far as I know, there are no children there. There's nothing but evil and death in that place." Mag brushed aside a tear and forced a smile. "The little girl, Eliana, is she safe?" She followed Gwen's gaze out the glass doors.

"I think so." Across the parking lot, Gwen watched the sun dip behind the buildings. "I hope so."

Cellar Doors

50

The sun retreated behind the hills, taking its warmth and leaving nothing but a thin, red crest in its wake. Cold seeped through cracks in the walls like water in a sinking ship. Sheriff Roy nudged his head under Gerri's arm and eased her from the chair.

"It's okay. I'm helping you to the floor."

Her leg muscles were cramped and locked in a sitting position. She moaned as he rolled her to her side and pulled his sports coat over her shoulder.

"Listen, I'm going back to my car to call for help. I need you to hang on. I'll be right back."

She didn't respond, and Roy could tell by her breathing that she wouldn't last the night, maybe not even the next hour. He placed his police radio next to her head and tucked the coat around her the best he could. He touched her cheek. She was freezing to death. "This jacket isn't good enough," he whispered.

He pulled his revolver from its holster and popped the shells from the cylinder. Lining the six cartridges next to the flashlight, he dug the Leatherman from his pocket. He remembered watching a survival show on TV where a lost hunter used gunpowder from his rifle bullets to start a campfire. The sheriff used the pliers on his multi-tool to twist the hollow point bullets from their shell casings. He ripped a strip from his cotton undershirt and placed it on the floor to collect the gunpowder.

"Okay." The sheriff looked around the room after emptying the shells. "I need kindling."

He limped behind the beam of his flashlight and collected debris from the kitchen and living room. Within minutes, he had gathered a pile of old wood and dry leaves. He chose the corner of the room farthest from Gerri and began positioning the scrap in the shape of a small teepee. At the base of the heap, he laced strips of his undershirt with gunpowder and brittle leaves.

His numb fingers shook slightly as he thoughtfully rolled two of the empty cartridges around in his hand. He cradled the shells and held them to his mouth, gently exhaling his warm breath. He sprinkled a pinch of gunpowder into each shell, hoping enough powder residue would stick to the condensation inside the casings. He shoved the shells back into the cylinder of his revolver. The primer button on the bottom of the shells was filled with a gas, that when struck by the firing pin, would create a spark. The spark should ignite the residue and then the pile of gunpowder.

Or the whole thing could blow up in my face. He squinted his eyes and crouched close to the trash heap, inhaling the mixed scents of gunpowder and earthly decay. Aiming the barrel at the gunpowder, he tried to recall what happened to the lost hunter from the TV show. He couldn't remember, but hoped he'd survived.

The flash from the muzzle ignited the powder, engulfing the debris in a ball of fire. The shock from the blast peppered his face and shirt with specks of burning powder.

Orange and blue-tipped flames peeked and darted through the creeping white smoke that boiled from the base of the debris. Dry leaves popped and crackled under the flame.

The sheriff grabbed his flashlight and hobbled to the bedroom door, glancing back at the still form of Gerri. Her silhouette danced on the wooden floor in the firelight. Already, the fire was slithering up the room's corner, twisting the old wallpaper into black curls.

"Burning faster than I thought it would," he swallowed the thick panic that had settled in the back of his throat.

Sheriff Roy pushed himself back through the broken window and dropped in a heap on the front porch. The forest was black and still. With his MagLite, he searched for the easiest path through the low limbs and heavy brush.

Behind him, the fire gurgled and snapped at the old wall studs. Pain raced up his leg, mingling with the dull ache from his hip. He surged ahead, high on fear and adrenaline, swatting twigs and briars that scratched at his face and snagged his clothes. The flashlight bobbed with each uneven step as he labored down the hill.

Again, he tried to occupy his mind with details. *Piece the facts together, Roy.* He began to mentally compartmentalize what he knew. JD had lied. Which sealed his guilt. And what about Gwen? Odds were good he was involved in kidnapping her, too.

Sheriff Roy stumbled from the tree-line and collapsed in the tall grass. He rolled to his back and sucked in the night air. Tears of exhaustion followed the lines of his crow's feet and slid toward his ears. His chest burned and pounded.

He staggered to his feet and dragged himself across the meadow to his car. The radio scanner squawked to life as he called dispatch. There was still an underlying fog of static, but the dispatcher's voice rang through.

"Claire, I need an ambulance and a fire truck at the old Potter's place immediately."

"10-4 Sheriff. On the way."

He switched the channel to his handheld and thumbed the mic. "Gerri, this is Sheriff Roy. I'm on the way with help." The sheriff dropped the mic and slid his twelve gauge from the console mount. He pulled himself around the side of the car to the trunk. Tossing tools and equipment on the ground, he came up with a metallic silver emergency blanket. Using his shotgun as a crutch, he pushed his way toward the burning skyline.

The radio's volume fluctuated. Hidden in the static was a wet rattling, like a congested chest. Fragmented words and phrases both screamed and whispered. Some were gentle; others spat obscenities.

Details.

The sheriff prided himself on his eye for details. But he had failed to notice one. The cellar doors were open. And darkness seeped from the cavity; a twisting and probing darkness.

51

Beth bolted the door and slid the safety chain. She took a quick glance through the peephole before turning to survey the motel room. Eliana sat on the nearest twin bed holding a Happy Meal toy. She was always smiling.

"How long can we stay here?" Her voice was small and squeaky.

"Not long." Beth smiled and ruffled her hair before swinging their suitcase to an empty chair. "Pretty soon we'll find our new home." She furrowed her eyebrows in a thoughtful expression. "What do you think about getting a puppy?"

Eliana's eyes lit up. "A puppy?" she squealed.

Beth pretended to consider the idea for a second. "Yep, I think we should definitely get a new puppy to go with our new home."

Eliana hugged her toy and rolled back, giggling on the bed.

Beth focused on the two small suitcases; the only possessions they were able to bring. She swallowed a sudden wave of emotion. She and Eliana would have to start over again, from scratch.

She knew it couldn't last forever, she and Eliana living in obscurity. One day, she would be forced to face her past sins. She felt that familiar tug inside. There was something she knew had to be done, but it saddened her to think about it. She tried pushing it out of her mind.

Trust Me.

Maybe the gentle voice was right. She had been wrong about Jude. What if she was wrong about this, too? She remembered reading that having untested faith was useless. This could be a chance to experience God's faithfulness through her action.

There's a phone in the lobby.

"I know there is," she quietly answered the voice in her heart.

But calling Eliana's birth mother didn't make any sense. And it certainly didn't fit the plans she had made for their future. If the tug in her heart was indeed God, then why was He trying to ruin her plans? Why would He ask her to give up what meant more to her than anything in the world?

Beth slowly circled the small motel room. It smelled like pine cleaner. *What if this is the best life I can offer her? Running from hideout to hideout; never able to settle. On the other hand, what can a young mother give her that I can't? Why would God ask me to give Eliana back to her?*

Be still.

Beth stopped pacing. *Either every promise is true, or none are. Either He is God of all, or God of nothing.* She watched Eliana play quietly. The child didn't worry about her future. Didn't question where her next meal would come from, or what she would wear when the small suitcase of clothes was no longer adequate. She simply trusted. She had a simple faith that her needs would be provided for. She was content.

"Faith of a child," Beth whispered. She remembered the phone in the lobby. Perhaps it was time to test her faith.

52

Kat locked the glass doors of the Movie Mania. Five minutes until closing time. She gathered a stack of movies from the overnight return bin and placed them on the front counter. She went through her nightly ritual systematically; her movements on autopilot.

But her thoughts were in another place. Haunted by the memory of the blonde-haired girl from earlier in the week. She remembered her delicate features, the smell of her perfume. Her laughter.

The voices stirred in Kat's head.

What did you do? they asked maliciously. *What did you do to the blonde girl?*

Kat counted out the cash register and zipped the day's earnings in a green bag with the tally receipt.

Where is she? What did you do to her? The voices jeered and prodded.

Kat tried to block them out, but found them impossible to ignore. She dropped the moneybag on the counter, staring at the empty register.

Where is she? What did you do? The voices were relentless.

She rubbed her forearm. Back and forth. Harder. Back and forth. The questions became a frenzy in her mind. She felt dampness seep through her sleeve. Back and forth. Back and forth. Warm blood stained her fingers.

"What have I done?" she whispered.

The memory played like a horror show in her mind.

She remembered watching the blonde girl leave the parking lot. Remembered jabbing the number and hearing the voice answer on the other end. The girl's account information was displayed on the computer screen. The rectangle cursor blinked next to her home address. The Group would be pleased.

She heard her own voice reply to the questions on the phone.

"Yes, she's alone. Parents will be gone for the week. No, no one will be with her tonight."

Kat remembered hanging up the phone, sealing the fate of the blonde-haired girl.

The voices rose and swayed. *Where is the girl?* they teased.

"She's gone now." Kat spoke to the empty register.

What did you do?

"She's gone away."

Is she safe now? The voices purred in her mind.

"No, she's not safe."

An empty movie case fell from a shelf in the horror section. Across the showroom, another case toppled from a shelf. Kat's vacant eyes were locked on the register oblivious to her surroundings. Lost in the swirling voices. Thin streaks of blood ran to her fingertips, swelling into perfect droplets before plunging to the carpet.

What did you do to her? the voices sang.

"I took away her perfect life," Kat whispered.

You're an evil girl, Black Kat. The voices hissed her name. *How could you let this happen?*

"I don't know." Kat lowered her head. Her pink strand of hair unwound and brushed her cheek.

You're an evil girl! Evil! Evil! The voices chanted in unison.

The words pounded in her head. Kat reached for her backpack, dumping its contents on the counter. Her phone blinked to life from the impact, displaying a 'MISSED CALL' message. Kat fished through the items, resting her fingers on her compact. She looked at the showroom. Numerous movie cases lay on the floor. She took the compact and walked around the counter toward the back.

You killed her, the voices moaned. *You killed the blonde girl.*

Kat reached the back wall and twisted the knob to the storage room. It was dark.

So evil. So worthless. So ugly. The voices continued. *You should have stopped your family from leaving. Should have gone with them. You could have saved them. But instead, you stayed behind. They died, and you lived. You killed them. Just like you killed the blonde girl. Just like you killed your baby.*

Each word was a blade, cutting deeper.

She felt her way across the room to another door. Gripping the compact, she reached for the doorknob. Her eyes welled with tears. She *was* an evil person. She had done terrible things. Unspeakable things. She twisted the doorknob and stepped into the restroom; the fluorescent light flickered and came to life. She placed the compact on the sink and met her reflection in the mirror. Black streaks of mascara trailed down her cheeks. Her hands shook slightly as she balled them into fists; the voices had settled to a murmur. They were waiting. For a moment, she savored the silence. The gentle hum of the fluorescent light. The steady throb of her heart. She watched her eyes in the mirror.

"I hate you," she whispered.

"I hate you." Her voice rose.

"I hate you!" Her voice rang in her ears. "I hate you!"

Kat clicked the compact open revealing the pearl-handled blade. She took her hateful friend in her bloodied fingers as the voices in her head moaned and laughed. She could hear movie cases hitting the floor in the showroom.

She had done evil things. Unspeakable things.

Tonight, she would quiet the voices.

Cellar Doors

53

J D left the hospital parking lot and snaked around the back roads. Dispatch reported that the cell phone was on the move.

He would follow Eric and find the child. It was that simple. No one else mattered. Just the girl. And now that the local Chapter had been dissolved, nothing would stop him from infiltrating the heart of the High Echelon. The girl was the key he needed. He would deliver her personally.

JD scanned the handful of parked cars around a warehouse of the water treatment facility. But why would they hide the child here?

"Odd behavior, hemming themselves in this dead-end park."

And a couple other things didn't add up. The Implement was missing. It had been sent to kill the woman and lead JD to the girl, but something had happened. The woman and girl were still lost, and the Implement was gone.

That had never happened.

It always killed or maimed its mark and returned the talisman to JD. Until now.

A hint of panic stirred his stomach. He slammed the steering wheel with his palms. It had taken years of sweat, tears and lots of blood, learning to control the Implement. And even now, theirs was a very shaky relationship. More like trying to catch a cobra in the dark. Controlling demons wasn't an exact science. JD rubbed the bite scar on the back of his neck, just below his hairline. A lesson he learned as a child. A lesson he learned well. He never turned his back to the demon again.

Fragmented shadows of his childhood boiled to the surface of his mind. JD had spent much of his life surrounded by spirits and the dead.

Before his foster family, he remembered growing up in the small house above Potter's Field with his brother and drunken father. JD was eight. His brother, thirteen. They were dirt poor, and always hungry. When their father's drinking became abusive, he and his brother would fend for themselves in the cave below the house. JD's brother hated the cave.

He called it the cellar.

The doors to the cellar were too heavy for JD to open by himself, so he would sit in front of them and wait for his brother to let him in. He knew the cave was different than other caves. It was a magical place. Not the cartoon kind of magic, with unicorns and candy. It was darker, full of strange noises.

And children.

His brother saw them too, but was scared of them. The children could float around and disappear when they wanted to. And some of the taller spirit children were hateful.

And very jealous.

They would tell JD that he was special, but they didn't like his brother. They would bite his brother and scratch his arms. At first, JD was scared of them too, but over time, he found comfort in their company. They would open the cellar doors when his brother wasn't there. And they would talk to him, tell him things. Sometimes, they would tell him secret things.

They would always play games; they loved games. Hide and seek was their favorite. Sometimes, they would play tricks on JD. Like hiding deep within the cave, farther than his candle would last if he tried to follow; and then call for him to find them. Sometimes, they would blow his candle out and then giggle as he sobbed in the darkness.

Sometimes, they would hide inside of him.

One night, while playing hide and seek, the spirits led his brother deep into the cave and left him there. The spirits told JD that his brother would never come back. And he never did.

His father blamed him for his brother's disappearance. "A wretched child, that's what you are. Nothing but a wretched child!"

The abuse was worse without his brother to fend for him. As a result, he spent more time in the cave with the spirits. They told him things about his father, too. Some of the bad things he had done; people he had hurt. Where he hid his gun. When his father was asleep, or too drunk to walk, the spirit children would come out of the cave and up to JD's room.

One night, they woke him to play a different kind of game. He cried at first, but they told him it would be okay; they would be his family now. They would take care of him and never leave him or forsake him. He remembered sneaking into his father's room; he remembered the thick smell of whiskey and vomit. The sight of his father passed out on his soiled bed. The spirits told JD where the handgun was, told him what to do. He found the gun; it was heavy and bulky in his hands. The metal was cool...

JD shined the patrol car's spotlight around the backside of a storage building. He weaved through the parking lot, looking for Eric's motorcycle. His attention was drawn to the chip transponder on the seat next to him. He had accounted for most of the flashing numbers on the screen, but there were still a couple more. "We're wasting precious time here," he growled at the transponder. It was becoming obvious he had been diverted. "Perhaps they're smarter than we thought."

Cellar Doors

54

"The sheriff's okay," Jude said. "We can trust him. I don't know about anyone else in the department, but he's honest. Beth has taken Eliana to the city, and Eric is keeping an eye on JD until the sheriff calls. So that leaves us."

Gwen didn't look convinced. "Jude, we can't just hide while Aunt Gerri is still missing. What if she comes home, or what if something has happened to her? What if she needs us?"

Mag slid her coffee cup to the end table. "I'll go back to the hospital," she said. "The Group has no reason to suspect me. And as far as JD knows, I'm no different than...before." She paused. "Besides, I can watch for your aunt if she's brought in."

"I don't think it's a good idea for any of us to be in the open," Jude said.

"It's just until your aunt is found." She lowered her voice. "Jude, it's the least I can do, considering the part I've played."

Jude thoughtfully watched the sun ebb behind Building D. "The police and SWAT will be focused on the cave. They'll find any children there." He looked at Mag. "Do you have any idea where JD lives?"

"Yes," Mag replied. She was about to ask why.

"What if Aunt Gerri's there?" Jude looked at Gwen. "Eric is tailing JD, so I'll know where he is at all times. I'll just drop by and check it out."

"You'll drop by and just break into a cop's house?" Gwen wasn't buying his nonchalance.

"Well, once JD is exposed for what he really is, I don't think they'll let him stay a cop."

"Right, so you're breaking into a psycho kidnapper's house. That makes me feel better."

"What if she's there, Gwen?"

"Okay, but you're not leaving me here alone," Gwen decided. The fear in her eyes softened his response. "Sure. We both go."

JD's house was in a quiet neighborhood. An established community of ranch-style homes and tall trees. They noticed the inside lights were off and the driveway was empty as they crept past the brick house. They parked Gwen's VW two houses up and turned off the headlights.

"Sure about this?" Jude asked, watching the house.

"It was your idea, remember?" Gwen touched his hand. "Before we do this, I want you to know I'm sorry about the other night. I got a little crazy and blew things out of proportion. I had no right to push you into a corner like that."

"Gwen, it was all me," Jude grinned. "I seem to have a gift of saying the exact opposite of what I mean. I really like you a lot, and just want you to be happy. Hopefully, your idea of happiness involves spending time with me."

"Fair enough," Gwen returned his smile. "I can work with that."

"So," Jude killed the motor, "you ready to do something stupid?"

"Lead the way."

Two large willow trees shadowed the back door. Weeping willows. Gwen decided they looked more like lanky tarantulas with their spindly branches sweeping the bare ground in unison.

Jude gently rattled the back door. "Locked."

Gwen looked over her shoulder for signs of life next door. "Guess you forgot your secret agent lock-picking set, huh?"

Jude hunched in front of the door and dug into his back pocket. "Think I can use a credit card," he mumbled optimistically, "or maybe my library card..."

A stone gargoyle sailed past Jude's head, shattering the rectangle of glass above the doorknob.

Jude jumped back, fumbling his library card.

Gwen reached into the dark hole and twisted the lock from the inside. She only smiled.

"Like you said, it's not like we're breaking into a cop's house now."

They stepped into the dark laundry room, crunching broken glass underfoot. The nearest doorway opened to the kitchen. "Wow, he keeps a clean house for a bad guy." Gwen tried to disarm her apprehension with sarcasm. The house was almost too clean.

Actually, it looked more staged than tidy. Like a house for sale. No warmth or signs of life. Just sterile shades of white and grey. The dining room was just as bland; a small table with one chair. They eased into the den. A ridged, leather recliner faced a plasma TV. Behind the chair, hung a generic print of a mountainscape and waterfall framed in curled gold. Perhaps the print was an attempt at warmth or atmosphere. But it just came off as creepy and out of place.

They passed a bedroom. Twin-sized bed. Night table. Lamp. Pristine and unused.

The second bedroom door was locked from the inside.

Gwen glanced at Jude. Sweat beaded his top lip; he could feel it, too. A strip of pale light bled from under the door. He pressed his ear against it and listened, finally shaking his head. "I don't hear anything," he whispered.

Gwen's eyes wandered back to the shadowed den. Back to the creepy picture. "Maybe we should just go." The sarcasm had left her voice.

Jude skimmed the top of the door casing with his fingers, smiling nervously when the hunch produced a key.

The door opened to a cluttered office. A metal desk took up most of the room. A worn cot hunched in a corner and a floor-to-ceiling bookshelf crowded the southern wall. Its bowed shelves strained under the weight of rows of old books. The single window in the room was masked by black plastic.

Gwen noticed a collection of stone gargoyles surrounding the room. Perched on the bookshelf. Sitting on the desk. Squatting in the corners. Their sapphire eyes radiated the lamplight, their flickering tongues frozen in grinning faces. She frowned at the nearest one.

The wall across from the bookshelves held sections of corkboard covered with a collage of scrap paper. News clippings surrounded a network of snapshots. Gwen studied the pictures while Jude moved to the desk. Some of the photographs were dated. A few looked pretty old. The first photo focused on the license plate of a car; the next was a blurry shot of a man stepping out of a building. Below it and stapled to a picture of a teenage girl, was a receipt from the Movie Mania.

Gwen leaned closer to the bottom row of photos; she recognized the yellow strands of police tape fencing a hospital room door. A series of crime scene photos. She recognized Eric's friend, Josh. The first picture displayed him lying sideways in his hospital bed; his eyes were open, and his chest was torn—she looked away. She'd never seen a dead body like this.

Unlike TV crime shows, where the faces and gore were always blurred, these photos were raw and unapologetic. Her eyes darted to the next picture before she could stop them. It was a close-up of a man's face. His eyes were cloudy, locked in a dead stare. Gwen caught her breath—the same silver necklace was draped across his nose and mouth. She felt the fingers of fear brush the back of her soul. She shuddered. "Jude, I'm ready to get out of here."

Jude tipped over a crouching gargoyle as he sifted through a stack of folders. "Yep, just a sec," he said automatically. On the desk's corner, a leather-bound book weighed down a jumble of loose papers. The worn spine read *Demonology*. A second book bristled with paper bookmarks. It was open, with entire paragraphs underlined in red. He scanned the first paragraph:

[...1978, David Seeton, a British geophysicist, compiled data on silicon dioxide compounds found in the basalt and andesite formations of the dormant Mauna Kea volcano. Further studies detected signs of microbial activity normally found...]

"I don't think there's anything here we can use to find Aunt Gerri. And I don't know what this guy's involved in, but I'm sure it's not good." Jude scanned a couple more paragraphs:

[...discovered an underground void. Unlike the expected magma chamber, we found an open pocket that expanded beneath the surface deeper than our equipment could reach...]

"Riveting," Jude mumbled, skipping to the picture at the bottom.

A cross section of the Earth was dissected into layers. He read the bold print:

[Five Layers of Earth: *The earth's crust is at the thickest point less than fifty miles deep and is comprised of alumino-silicates and rock and quartz compounds. The upper and lower mantles at eighteen hundred miles are comprised mostly of Ferro-magnesium silicates and poisonous gases. The outer core is a liquid nickel-iron alloy. The inner core is molten...]*

He skipped to a scribbled footnote:

[There are six known shafts leading to the earth's core.]

Next to the red center of the Earth was an arrow. Connected to the arrow was the word 'HELL', in red sharpie.

Jude studied the picture. "Kind of gives the whole *hell on earth* an interesting twist." He picked up the manila folder next to the book. Connected to the folder by paperclip was a map of Willow. A red circle highlighted an area outside of town. Written next to the circle was:

Akeldama—shaft number four. Cellar Doors.

"Looks like the location of the cave," Jude whispered to himself. "He thinks the cave in Potter's Field is an entrance to Hell?"

Jude flipped open the folder. It took a minute for him to realize what he was looking at. A torn piece of notebook paper held four names.

The color drained from his face. "Gwen, you need to see this."

He scrolled through the names on the paper, the names of four of the Six Seats. He didn't recognize most of them. But one name caught his breath.

55

J udas slid his knife under the windowpane, scoring the paint
that held it shut. Through the lavender curtains, he could
see into her bedroom.

It was quiet.

A strip of soft light seeped from under the closed door, but
otherwise, the room was dark. Judas positioned his hands
against the top of the windowsill and pushed upward. The
window creaked and popped, giving slightly. He wiped damp
palms on his jeans; the anticipation was almost overwhelming.
He took a few short breaths, trying to calm his excited heart.

Smiling, he pushed the windowsill again.

With an obstinate crack, it relented and slid freely up.
Warm air and the sweet fragrance of her room drifted from the
opening. His heart pounded faster. Carefully, so carefully, he
brushed the curtains to the side and waited.

Watching.

Nothing moved.

To the left, a small bed was littered with stuffed animals. In
the midst of the animals, he could make out the still form of
Eliana under the blankets. Above the bed, a small butterfly
clock clicked rhythmically.

With a fluid motion, he pushed himself onto the sill and
dropped into the room. Crouching in the moonlight, he waited
for his eyes to adjust. His heart beat steadily in his throat. He
had been so careful, so attentive to details.

Now everything was falling into place. He couldn't help but smile in the dark as he stood, casting his lanky shadow over the bed. Blonde hair lay scattered across the pillow. He slid the knife out and reached for the blanket.

"How's it going, buddy?"

Eric limped from a corner shadow. A Louisville Slugger baseball bat hung loosely at his side. Judas spun to face Eric, his expression twisted in shock.

"Stay there, or I kill her! I swear, I'll kill her!" Judas held the knife over the mound on the bed.

"Mistake," Eric said calmly, gripping the bat with both hands. "Big mistake."

Judas jerked the blanket back, revealing a stuffed teddy bear crowned with a blonde hair extension. He cursed with the realization he had been set up. The baseball bat caught him in the midsection.

"Ooophf!" Judas sagged into a heap, gasping for air.

Eric took a step closer, the bat resting across his shoulder. "Thought you might show up here, JD. You're actually pretty predictable."

The knife glinted in the moonlight, slicing the air in front of Eric's face. The bat swung again, catching JD below the left ear with a dull crunch. The force of the swing took him head-first through the lavender curtains. He hit the ground hard; glass and chunks of wood cascaded around him.

"Not much fun being thrown through a window, is it?" Eric leaned against the jagged window opening.

JD rolled to his back with a sigh. A trickle of blood slid from his ear. "You do know I'm going to kill you, right?" he hissed.

Eric wiped the Slugger on his blue jeans. "Hey, I can do this all night if you can."

56

"What is it?" Gwen took the folder from Jude. The heading was scrawled across the top of the page in cursive: *Six Seat Hierarchy*. She mouthed the names as she read: Dr. Vic Keenan, Dr. Gail Morrah, Rev. Ferrell Collins, Gerri Coe... She read the name again. Her stomach fell.

"Aunt Gerri?" She looked at Jude.

Jude was already moving. "We need to leave."

"This can't be right, Jude." She focused on a gargoyle squatting near her feet. "She can't be part of this."

Something bumped against a wall in the den. Gwen heard it first.

Jude reached for her hand. "We need to find Eric. He doesn't realize what we're mixed up in." Jude tucked the manila folder under his arm and cracked the door open. He waited for his eyes to adjust to the dark house. The central unit kicked on, rustling the den's drapes. "Just the heater making noise," he whispered. But was unsure.

Gwen's attention was still on the gargoyle. Its sapphire eyes glowed in the room's light. She couldn't shake a familiar stirring inside.

"Okay, stay close," Jude said, leading her into the short hallway.

The brood of gargoyles watched as they left the room.

Gwen gripped Jude's hand and pulled him closer. The den was quiet and seemed darker than before. Headlights from a passing car sent shadows skirting around the room. They rounded the dining room threshold and tiptoed to the kitchen.

Jude cupped his flashlight to the floor and directed the beam toward the laundry room. "As soon as we're outside, run straight to the car…"

"Please," a muffled voice pleaded from the rear of the house, "please help me."

Gwen sucked in a sharp breath. "A little girl." She looked at Jude.

"Please help me, Gwen."

"Wait." Jude squeezed her hand. "It's not right."

"She called my name. What if it's Eliana? What if JD found her, or maybe another child he's taken…"

"Gwen." Jude spoke softly but with confidence. "I don't know what that is, but it's not a child."

Gwen glanced back at the den. The shadow from the passing car had settled, but something was still stirring.

For a moment, she was huddled in the cave again, listening to the child cry in the darkness. Helplessness seeped around her soul. She remembered the piercing eyes and guttural language that came from Mag.

She remembered the fear.

Gwen had always been plagued by fears, but nothing like this. This fear was alive. She swallowed the heartbeat rising in her throat. As a child, her mother would assure her there was nothing to fear but fear itself. But Gwen knew that wasn't true. There was a fear worried mothers couldn't explain or wish away. A fear that fed on childhood imagination. A fear that could see you in the dark.

A fear that could touch you.

They followed the flashlight beam through the kitchen and into the laundry room. Shards of broken glass winked as they approached. Hunched in front of the door was the stone gargoyle Gwen had used to break in. It was sitting upright like a small animal; its eyes reflected the light.

"Jude?" Gwen squeezed his arm, unable to breathe.

Jude paused, "It's okay, Gwen. We'll not be intimidated by flower garden decorations." He pushed the stone statue aside with his foot and opened the back door. "We need to find Eric and the sheriff."

Cellar Doors

57

Roy's eyes were locked on the glow at the top of the hill. He leaned heavily against the shotgun, plunging the barrel into the cold earth as he limped along. Tears came to his eyes with each step, and his heart burned with each breath.

The wind kicked up as he trudged on. *A few more yards and I'll be able to see the house.* His imagination plagued him with scenes of Gerri's charred body lost in the rubble. He pushed the thoughts away. *Maybe she was able to pull herself from the inferno.* A cough of wind chattered through the leaves of a nearby elm. He glanced at the treetops; the wind would spread the fire. *Got to hurry.*

The backside of the house was a solid wall of fire; the roofline was completely lost in boiling smoke. The sheriff stumbled up the steps, dropping his flashlight and shotgun. Heat from the porch window blew across his face in smoky waves. Each breath sliced his lungs like a knife, stabbing at his heart. Flames licked the top of the windowsill, lapping up the rotten wood in hungry gulps.

Through the window, he watched the blanket of fire caress exposed rafters. Embers swirled and dropped from the ceiling, sizzling into plumes of dark smoke. Pulling himself to the window, he held his breath and toppled into the living room. The roar of the fire was deafening as he crawled across the floor. A barrier of smoke surrounded the room, burning his eyes as he blinked back tears. He pulled the edge of his shirt over his mouth and nose and crawled to the bedroom door. Fire cascaded around his head, singeing his clothes.

Gerri's motionless body lay on the floor. The fire had traveled up the wall and was dissecting the roof over her head. The ceiling sagged over the room, moments before collapse.

Her face was hot to touch; her skin looked raw and sunburned. He checked her pulse.

The air in the room was thick; the smoke inching closer to the floor. He pulled off his flannel shirt and tied it around her head. "You've got to help me, Gerri," he yelled over the roar. "I can't carry you." Gerri rolled her head toward his voice. Coughing violently, she cracked an eye open.

Above their heads, the ceiling creaked as the house shuddered in its final throes of death. Sheriff Roy locked his arms around her and leaned against her dead weight, dragging her toward the room's window.

He propped her against the smoldering wall, hooked her leg at the knees, and pushed her body against the pane. It squeaked a complaint before bursting like a shimmering dam.

Outside, he pulled her body as far from the fire as his ebbing strength would allow. Collapsing next to her, he closed his eyes and listened to the flames squeal as they consumed the house.

It almost sounded like children singing.

"Sheriff?"

Sheriff Roy rolled to his back. His head pounded in sync with his hip. He squinted at the light being shined in his eyes. "Get that light out of my face," he rasped, allowing his thoughts to untangle. A face leaned over him mouthing words. The mumble became sentences. An EMT was probing and prodding his chest.

"Can you hear me, Sheriff?"

He was aware of the heat from the house. It was mostly charred remnants on a bed of bright coals, now. Sounds of voices drifted from the perimeter, extinguishing scattered fires. "Yeah, I can hear you." His body was sore. "Help me up, son."

"We've got a cot on the way, Sheriff. Just lie here for a couple more minutes."

Roy straightened his leg and tested his hip. "Help me up, son. I'm not riding a cot." He remembered Gerri. "Is the woman okay?"

"We took her down already. She's roughed up pretty bad; looks like smoke inhalation and dehydration. She'll pull through, though."

The sheriff grunted to a sitting position. "Is she talking? Did she say what happened to her?"

"I don't think so, Sheriff. We put her on oxygen to clear her lungs. The smoke almost did her in." The EMT checked his pupils with the penlight again. "Do you know how the fire started?"

Roy blinked at the light. "Yeah, I know how it started."

Cellar Doors

58

E ric wrapped a third loop of duct tape around Judas' hands. He was lying on the ground, surrounded by broken glass. Blood dripped from a hateful gash in front of his ear, and he wasn't speaking.

"I just don't get it, JD. What do you have against me and my sister? We don't know you. We've never done anything to hurt you."

Judas grimaced and worked his jaw back and forth. His head was throbbing and growing stiff from the bat assault. He rolled his eyes to find Eric. "You think I care about you?" He spat blood. "You're nothing but a stepping stone. Just a pawn to be sacrificed for my greater good." He chuckled in spite of the pain. "You're nothing to me."

"I know all about your sick club; your High Echelon. I know what you do to children."

Judas met his eyes. "I doubt you know as much as you think about a great many things. You believe selling children is all I care about?" He tried rolling to his side. "You're not much of a big picture guy, are you?"

"So why my sister?" Eric's face grew dark.

Judas offered him a crooked smile. "Your sister's a different story. She has worth. She has...potential."

Eric drew the smiling Judas close to his face, "I'll not let you hurt my sister again. That I promise you."

Judas coughed a clot of blood. His breath was laced with sulfur. "And remember what I promised you, Gunslinger."

59

Emergency Physicians Hospital

ag scrolled through the patients on her clipboard. Gerri Coe's name wasn't there, but the ICU was busier than usual—and it was still early. It was like the whole town was coming unhinged. A handful of car accidents, a domestic dispute turned violent, an attempted suicide.

She followed the hallway past rooms of devastated lives; room after room of suffering people. Usually, she hated the night shift. On good nights, she felt a sort of detached pity for them. Most of the time, she simply felt indifferent.

But tonight, while following her routine of administering medication and monitoring vitals, she was introduced to a new emotion.

Compassion.

For the first time, her eyes were opened to the realization of the heartache around her. Each room held a life with a network of experiences and influence. Each bed held a desperate soul teetering on the edge of eternity by sterile tubes and bandages. Tonight, some family trees would heal and grow stronger; others would shrivel and vanish forever.

Mag pushed her cart next to the nearest door and checked her clipboard. Attempted suicide. A young girl.

She could relate. The world turns so slowly for the depressed. Having lived so close to darkness herself, made coming into the light that much brighter.

Kat awoke to the medical beeps of a hospital monitor. She lay in bed facing sterile walls. The inky night colored the window behind slanted blinds. Her drug-induced grogginess dissipated, slowly bringing her surroundings into focus. Her arms were bandaged from the elbows down. They were sore. How long had she been here? Her eyes followed a single tube that looped and spiraled from her left hand to a drip above her head. Though the room was quiet, she could sense the swirling voices in the back of her mind. They were still there. Waiting.

She could feel their whispers. *You have failed*, they chided her. *You can't do anything right*. Maybe they were right. She couldn't even end the pain.

A warm tear gathered and fell from her eye. Her life had no meaning. No future. She was so tired. She just wanted it all to stop. She looked at her arms again. *Would killing myself be the answer?* She didn't really want to die. She just didn't want to live like this.

The door opened to a woman with strawberry hair.

"Good evening, Beautiful. How are you feeling?"

Kat considered the question for a moment. The appropriate answer was to lie and say everything was fine. But she was tired of lying. Tired of the perpetual charade.

"I'm not really doing so good," she heard herself say. Another tear strayed.

The woman paused.

"I'm not doing good at all," Kat continued. "And I'm tired of not doing good."

The woman settled at the foot of the bed. "I think I understand." She set aside her clipboard, giving Kat her full attention. "Maybe I can help."

"I sort of doubt that," Kat said in a small voice. "Nobody knows what I've done."

The woman rested her hand on Kat's foot. "You can tell me."

Kat felt warmth in her voice. Maybe she would listen. Maybe she could help. Something stirred in Kat that she hadn't felt in a long time.

She breathed it in with a deep sigh as tears fell freely.

"Okay," Kat managed to say.

"Good. I'm Mag."

"My name is Katrina."

Cellar Doors

60

"Duck your head," Sheriff Roy warned about two seconds too late. Judas winced as his head thumped against the rim of the squad car. He shuffled himself to the center of the backseat. "Hope the cuffs aren't too tight," the sheriff mumbled, slamming the car's door.

Eric waited outside the driver's side window as the sheriff switched off the blue lights. "You hurt, son?" he asked Eric.

"I'm fine, but you may want to have his jaw looked at. I might have broken it."

The sheriff glanced in the rear-view mirror. "He'll be fine," he growled. The sides of his neck flushing.

Judas' eyes were locked on Eric. His lips curled in a slight grin.

"The lady and kid who live here," the sheriff nodded at the house, "they okay?"

Eric returned Judas' stare. "They're safe now," he said under his breath.

"Good. I want to see everybody in my office in an hour. The woman, the girl, your sister and Jude. You bring them all in. Don't talk to anyone else, just me. You got it?"

"Yeah. I got it."

Judas watched the sheriff's eyes in the rear-view mirror as they pulled away from Eric. He said nothing, but his mind raced through a number of rehearsed scenarios. He couldn't help but smile slightly; he had thought of everything, even this. There was always a contingency plan just in case things got a little off track. He had been surprised once—well, twice. He flexed his swelling jaw; *didn't expect the gunslinger to be waiting in the girl's room with a baseball bat.*

"Smells like you've been to Hell and back, Sheriff." Sheriff Roy glanced at the rear-view mirror. "JD, you have no idea what you're in for. Just shut up and sit back."

Judas smiled as he slid his hand into the crevice of the seat. His fingers searched the tight crease until... *finally, there it is.* A sliver of masking tape covered a single handcuff key stowed in the crease of the backseat. He tried not to smile, but couldn't help it. He had thought of everything.

Judas waited until they turned onto Highway 110, a curvy two-lane road with lots of pine and willow trees. Plenty of cover. Plenty of places to hide a body. Satisfied, he rolled his eyes back in his head and slowly slid to the floorboard.

"Sheriff, something's wrong." Judas' voice quaked as he jerked and convulsed.

Sheriff Roy craned his neck to see. "You'll be fine, JD. I'm not stopping."

"Sheriff!" Judas bit the insides of his cheeks and pushed his face against the cage; bright blood streamed from his mouth. "Help me!"

Roy locked the brakes and slammed the patrol car into park. "I don't care if you're about to internally combust; I'm not loosening those cuffs." Roy slid his revolver out and hobbled to the back door.

When the door opened, Judas twisted and planted his foot in the center of the sheriff's chest. "I've already seen that happen, Sheriff. Believe me, it's not a pretty sight."

The sheriff rolled down the embankment with a grunt. Judas picked up the sheriff's service revolver and followed him.

"Time to go back to Hell, Sheriff." Judas aimed at Roy's head and pulled the trigger.

61

K at settled on the edge of the pier overlooking Swine Lake. The pier's ivory paint was blistered and curled, exposing the dingy rust primer beneath. From a distance, the staggering dock resembled a bleached skeleton jutting out over the water.

She watched as the cold waters tugged the dying sun deeper into its placid bowels. Her mind sorted through the last few hours. Tears slid down her cheeks, tracing the cracks and splits in the planks before dropping into the lake. She took a deep breath and opened her left hand. Her father's hobby knife mirrored the light from the water.

She searched the horizon for approval.

She had not been able to stop the pain before. Not been able to find release from the guilt. Not been able to quiet the swirling voices. She was so tired of living this lie; tired of the shame. She considered the blade in her hand; it was finally time to end this failed attempt of a life.

Another tear fell into the lake.

Kat swung her feet back and forth, feeling the icy water brush her toes. She held her breath as the blade touched her wrist. It was always cool against her skin. It always stung a little at first. She pressed down, feeling the familiar throb of her heart against the blade. She watched her blood swell from the cut. Letting out a deep breath, she pushed the corner of the blade deeper.

The drowning sun shimmered across the water as it sank beneath the inky crest. Every day was destined to end. Just as every life ended in death. Dust to dust. She and the day would die together.

Kat braced herself and stood, swaying gently, a little dizzy from the puncture. A thin streak ebbed down her hand, dissipating into cloudy droplets in the water. She smiled in the fading dusk and opened her hand again. Next to the stained blade was a grain-sized metallic chip.

"This life is over," she whispered, tossing the pearl-handled blade and the tracking device into the lake. She watched the ripples roll across the glassy surface.

Mag stepped from behind and touched Kat's shoulder, handing her a paper towel.

"I'm free now." Kat smiled at Mag and held the towel against her wrist. "I'm really free now."

The swirling voices were gone. Her old life had ended.

As the sun dissolved into the lake, Mag helped Katrina sort through past regrets.

"For one, I don't want to be called Kat anymore; I don't want that identity to shadow me." Katrina searched the limbs of her oak tree. It sheltered them like an old friend. No crows watched from twisted branches today; no accusers to hurl insults.

Telling Mag her secrets was the hardest thing she had ever done. Admitting her dependence on the blade had been difficult, but Mag had not judged. Only listened. When Katrina whispered her involvement with the Group, Mag couldn't hide her shock. Or her tears. Mag relayed her own past, and they found a measure of comfort in one another's pain. Katrina told Mag about her baby. Her lovely child sacrificed in fear and consumed by greed. The guilt was still sharp and jagged as she resurrected the memory of her little girl. The best Mag could do was pray with her, hoping a God who knew all things may have intervened and shown mercy without anyone knowing to ask Him for it.

"What will you do now?" Mag asked.

"I don't know. I don't want to stay in Willow. I can't stay here, there are just too many memories." Katrina watched the oak's arms sway. "I had a missed call from the woman who took my baby. She tried to call me the night I attempted to..." her voice trailed a dark path.

"Why would she call me now? What more could she possibly want from me?"

"Perhaps the authorities would be interested in speaking with her," Mag replied.

"I'm sure they would. But I keep wondering if maybe she has news about my baby." Katrina touched the bandages on her wrists. "You know, I never even gave my little girl a name." She lowered her gaze from the tree to Mag. "But last night, I dreamed I was holding her again."

Cellar Doors

62

Jude stood in Mag's apartment, flipping between news channels. The usually sleepy town of Willow was fast becoming the top story in the state. The media was camped in front of the sheriff's station feeding on the tantalizing rumors of a corrupt small-town deputy and a string of unexplained deaths.

Mag and Eric had both arrived separately about ten minutes earlier. They were in the dining room together. Jude couldn't tell how it was going yet; this was the first time they had been together since the altercation in the cave.

"You know, I should be pretty mad at you." Eric didn't smile. "One minute, you're in my living room kissing me and offering to help find my sister. And the next, you're stabbing me with a stake. Not exactly the help I was looking for."

Mag blushed. "Eric, I'm not even sure what to say. I'm sorry seems a bit inadequate."

Eric tried to maintain a serious face, but couldn't help finding her obvious discomfort slightly amusing.

"Well, did you make up your mind?"

She looked like she might cry. "Make up my mind?"

"You really can't have it both ways, you know. Either you like me or you want to kill me."

Her mouth opened, but nothing came out.

"Jude told me you had a *come to Jesus* moment, or something. Said you were different, and not to take you trying to kill me so personal." Eric couldn't help but smile. "I guess that's easy to say if you've never had a woman come at you with a railroad spike."

"Actually, I attacked him with it, too," Mag whispered sheepishly.

"No kidding!?" Eric couldn't hide his surprise. "You got him, too? You *have* been busy."

She dropped her head in defeat. "Eric, I *am* so sorry. And yes, it's true. I am different. "And no, I..." she sniffed. "I don't want to kill you now."

Eric was still smiling. "Well, that's a start."

Mag realized he was playing with her. She wanted to smile, but felt guilty doing so. "I really don't think it's that funny," she finally said. "Can I see what I did?" She changed the subject.

He looked at her suspiciously.

It was her turn to laugh. "I'm not going to hurt you; I just want to see how bad it looks."

Eric rolled his pant leg up past the calf. The wound was still wrapped in gauze. "You can't really see anything, but trust me, it's not the worst injury I've acquired over the past couple days."

She turned her attention to his arm, touching the stitches that peeked from beneath his sleeve. "What about these?" she asked.

Eric rolled his sleeve above the Celtic cross. "They don't hurt, but they burn a little sometimes."

Mag traced the four rows of stitches with her fingers. "Could be an infection."

"I don't think so; it's different. The feeling kind of comes and goes. Like when I was with you in the cave. Right before you...tried to *help* me with that stake, the stitches started burning. And when I was alone with JD at Gwen's house, I remember them burning there, too."

Mag's hand rested in the crook of his elbow. "These scratches are from the demon. The sensitivity you feel may be spiritually connected."

"What, they only burn when the devil is near? I think that's a little far-fetched. I've never really believed in spiritual connections."

"But you believe now?"

Eric noticed she still held his arm cradled in hers. "I'm not sure what I believe." He tugged the sleeve back down. "Actually, if it's true these scratches can warn me of evil, well, they may just come in handy." The smile crept across his face again. "They don't feel funny now, so maybe you're okay after all."

She squeezed his arm and returned the smile. "So, I don't make you feel funny anymore?" It was her turn to tease.

Eric cleared his throat. "Well, that's not exactly what I meant," he mumbled.

"Eric," Gwen was calling from the kitchen. "Come listen to this."

"I'm not finished with you." Eric smiled at Mag. "Stay put."

Cellar Doors

63

"Gwen, baby, it's Aunt Gerri. Listen, this may be hard for you to hear; but for the last couple of days, I've been held against my will by a bad person. I know you've been worried, but everything's okay now. Call me as soon as you get this message, and please don't worry. I've talked with the sheriff, and I'm fine now. I'll be home soon."

Gwen slid her cell phone closed.

"I don't know what to say to her." Gwen looked at her brother.

"What if she finds Beth and Eliana?" Mag asked. "As a member of the Hierarchy, your aunt will know Beth; but Beth won't know her."

"As connected as these people are, I doubt a fake name at a Motel 6 will keep them off her trail for long." Eric stood. "I'll put her and the kid on a bus and get them out of the state."

"Wait, Eric," Gwen said. "If Beth can connect the Group to the stolen children or Josh's death, wouldn't she be valuable to the investigation?"

"She would, but she doesn't trust the authorities; she doesn't trust anybody. I don't think she'll take a chance with the child's safety. "

Jude joined the others. "They just reported finding an empty ambulance. It was a few blocks from the emergency room entrance. The driver and the assisting EMT are missing, too." Jude read the puzzled look on Gwen's face.

"The ambulance was coming from Potter's Field. Your aunt was in it."

"She left Gwen a message, Jude." Eric spoke up. "If what she said is true, she's on her way home now. Which will give me time to get Beth and Eliana to safety."

"What about the sheriff? Don't you think we should check in with him first?" Jude asked.

"I don't know if we should trust him, Jude. What if he and JD are in this thing together?"

"Eric, the more we're out in the open, the more chances something will go wrong. At least for now everyone's safe."

"Think about it, Jude, there are six seats in the Chapter. We only know the identities of four. There are still two unknown bad guys floating around out there; probably looking for Eliana this very minute. Maybe the sheriff's okay, or maybe the evil is more rooted than we thought." Eric moved to the door. "I'll be back in less than an hour."

"At least bring them here, Eric," Jude said. "Gwen's right. If we let Beth disappear again, more children could be hurt. The Group will just restructure and start over somewhere else. Maybe she can help stop them for good."

"I'll talk to her, Jude. But if she decides to disappear, I'm putting her on a bus."

Mag grabbed her jacket.

"No," Eric said, dismissing her intentions with a quick finger. "You and I don't make a very good team."

"Eric, I know the fear she feels. I understand her mistrust. We were part of the same evil, and we've both been set free from it. If I can just talk to her, maybe I can convince her to stop running. Or, at least, come here and talk to the authorities first."

Eric leaned against the door, favoring his wounded leg. "I like you, Mag. But I don't really trust you. How do I know you won't change your mind again?"

"Eric, I get it. And I don't blame you. But the benefit outweighs the risk. I didn't connect the pieces before, but there's something different about that little girl. She's not like the others. They want her too badly. Judas wants her too badly. There's a bigger plan in motion here; I think it's bigger than any of us. She's special, Eric." Mag allowed herself a quick smile. "Besides, look at you. You can barely stand on your own. Whether you trust me or not, I think you need me to lean on."

Cellar Doors

64

"Hi. I'm sorry to bother you. I'm Kat…" She attempted a smile. "Um, I mean, Katrina; from the Movie Mania. I checked you out the other day." Self-consciousness tugged at the corners of her smile.

The blonde-haired teenager propped against the door and crossed her arms to shield against the cold. Confusion wrinkled her forehead. "Wait. It's not due back yet, is it? I thought I rented it for like, three days."

"Oh, no. I'm not here for your movie." Katrina rubbed the fresh bandages under her hoodie sleeve. "I just needed to talk to you about something."

"You need to talk to me?"

"Yeah. You see, I made a mistake when you were in the store." She rubbed the bandages again. "No. Mistake is the wrong word," she whispered to herself. "I don't know an easy way to say this…"

A drop of blood slipped from the bandages, landing on the porch.

They both saw it.

"Are you bleeding?" Repulsion laced her confusion.

"No. I mean, yes; but it's okay. My arms are healing. I shouldn't be rubbing them."

Another drop followed.

Katrina tucked her arms behind her back and took a deep breath. "You're in danger. There are some people—some bad people, coming here for you."

The blonde girl shot a glance down the street. The block hummed with normal neighborhood sounds. She focused on the blood congregating around Katrina's feet. "What are you talking about?"

"I gave your address to some people. I'm really sorry I did it, and...I was in a bad place, then." Katrina's chin began to quiver. "I'm about to leave town for good, but I had to warn you; to tell you to leave, too." She blinked tears.

The blonde girl tightened her arms against a new chill.

"Is this a joke? Because it isn't funny. And why are you bleeding?"

Another drop plunged to Katrina's shoe and rolled to the porch. "You told me your parents are in Gulf Shores. Can't you just go find them?" Katrina whispered.

"You're starting to freak me out." The girl glanced down the street again. "I think you need to leave. Just get off my porch and leave."

Katrina wiped her eyes with the back of her hand. "I have some money; enough for gas or a bus ticket." She squatted over her backpack and dug into a side pocket. "Just go to Gulf Shores and find your parents. You'll be safe with them."

"Okay, this is getting too weird. I'm calling the cops, right now—"

"You can't call the cops!" Katrina found the blonde girl's eyes. "The cops won't help you." Her plea was strained. "Just take this and go find your parents." A wad of crumpled bills jutted from her fist. They were smeared with her blood.

The blonde girl looked as though she would vomit. "What kind of freak are you?"

"I know," she confessed. "I know I was a bad person." Katrina apologized with blurry eyes. "But I'm trying my best to fix the things I've done." She straightened the money and wiped away the smudge of blood. "Please, just find your parents."

"I don't want your money. And I don't want you bleeding on my porch." The blonde girl tried to mask her fear with anger.

Katrina's voice rose in desperation, "You don't understand. These people will hurt you!" She grabbed the blonde girl's shoulders and tightened her grip. "They will come here, and they'll take you away. You'll never see your parents or anyone you love again!"

The blonde-haired girl couldn't disguise her fear any longer. "Please, just leave me alone," her voice cracked.

Katrina softened. "I promise I won't hurt you. Just tell me you'll leave," she stepped away from the girl. "See, I won't hurt you. Just find your parents and stay with them."

Blood stained the girl's shoulders. All she could do was nod her head. "Okay."

"I'm so sorry," Katrina whispered again. "I just can't let you be taken from your family."

Cellar Doors

65

Eric pulled into the parking lot of the Motel 6. "They're in room seven," he nodded toward the stirring blinds. "We'll pick them up and go straight back to your place." He glanced at the rearview mirror apprehensively.

"Is your arm burning?" Mag asked.

"No," he scanned the parking lot. "But I don't need burning scratches to convince me we're in danger here."

Two suitcases were packed and waiting patiently near the door. Beth was nervous; obviously in a hurry to leave.

"Eric, we're ready, but I need to make a stop first. There's a girl I need to..." Her request was cut short at the sight of Mag.

"Who's this?"

"I'm Mag Dillon. I know who you are, Beth. I know about you and the child you have."

"Why would you bring someone here, Eric? I don't know this woman. Why would you endanger the life of Eliana like this?"

"It's not like that, Beth. Mag's a friend; she's safe." He winced hearing his own words. Maybe 'safe' was stretching it.

"I know about the High Echelon, Beth." Mag held her right wrist for Beth to see. A pink incision marked where the embedded microchip had been. "I was a Recruiter, too. And I met Eliana's birthmother; I know Katrina."

"You know Kat?" Beth's mistrust was seasoned with a shade of relief. "I tried contacting her." Beth's whisper was almost apologetic. "I intend to find her before leaving this place."

"She would like to see you. She's different now, Beth. She found a way out of the life she was trapped in. She found hope. She would like to meet her little girl."

"I've struggled with that decision. What if she can't care for the child? What about protection? If you know the Group, you know they'll kill them both."

Eric grabbed the nearest suitcase. "Beth, we can discuss this later. We need to go. Where's Eliana?"

Beth didn't respond. She was staring at the door.

"Eric!" Mag's whisper was urgent.

Gerri Coe stood in the doorway. Her face and hair were streaked with soot. Her clothes were torn and singed. She held the sheriff's shotgun.

"Aunt Gerri?" Eric's stomach dropped. "You followed me here?" He couldn't hide the betrayal in his voice.

"You were never supposed to be involved in any of this, Eric." She limped into the room and leveled the shotgun at Beth.

"This woman has our property. I just want the child back."

"That little girl is no one's property." Eric took a step closer. "Think about what you're doing. How could you do this to me? I'm family."

"Family?" Gerri didn't look at him. "I have no family."

The shotgun drifted toward Eric, keeping him at bay.

"I can't stop what this woman started," Gerri said. "She had no right to take what belonged to us."

"You dare speak of rights?" Beth was indignant. "Nothing we ever did was right. We ripped families apart; we destroyed lives and futures. That precious child has worth. She has purpose. And you will not interfere with her destiny."

"It's true the child has a purpose. And I will see it done, with or without your consent." Gerri's finger tightened on the trigger. "I will not ask again. Give her to me."

Beth slid her glasses off and folded them. "I can't do that," she said evenly.

"No. You're saying you won't do it." The shotgun trembled in her hands.

"Sweet ol' Aunt Gerri. Well, I'm certainly glad I didn't follow my gut instinct and blow your head off when I had the chance." Judas' lanky shadow filled the doorway behind Gerri. He stepped into the room, holding the cell phone transponder in one hand and a revolver in the other. "You actually became useful again." He sneered at Gerri before dropping the blinking phone.

Eric shifted his weight and nudged Mag to step behind him. Mag stiffened.

Judas surveyed the faces. "Won't you just look at all the sneaky rats bunched up in the same hole. You've all certainly made my hunt easier. Not as interesting, but easier." Judas scanned the room again. "But it seems we're missing the most important little rat. Where's the kid?"

"She won't tell me." Gerri's voice shook under her breath.

"That's because you didn't ask her the right way." Judas spat. "You should've gotten their attention right off the bat." He touched his bruised jaw and grinned at Eric. "Pardon the pun, Gunslinger."

Judas raised his revolver and fired in Eric's direction. The roar of the gun caused Gerri to nervously jerk the shotgun trigger. The impacted barrel cracked and mushroomed, blasting a chunk of paneling inches above Beth's head.

Eric engulfed Mag in his arms and dove with her to the floor.

Gerri swung the mangled shotgun barrel toward Judas and shot again. The room exploded with gunfire.

Judas slammed against the wall and staggered from the motel room, trailing a crimson streak. Gerri sank to her knees and slumped across the stock of the shotgun. A soft whimper passed her lips as a final breath left her lungs.

Beth crawled to Gerri and rolled her over, but she was already gone.

Eric shuffled to his knees; he was dizzy, and his stomach burned like fire. He touched the warm spot spreading around his left side. Mag had tried to push him away, but the bullet still clipped him.

Mag was lying next to him. He focused his attention on her. "I was trying to protect you."

She blinked at him, raising a hand to his face. "I know." Her chest was wet.

"Mag?" He could hear the confusion in his own voice, but it sounded detached, far away.

"Eric," she smiled as her eyes dimmed. "It's okay."

Eric grasped her hand and squeezed it against his face. *Too fast. This is happening too fast.*

"Mag, wait. Just hold on, I'll get help." *Please God, no.* The warmth of her hand slowly dissipated.

"Watch Eliana…" the instructions escaped with her final breath.

Her smile lingered a moment after her spirit left.

"Please, no." Eric pulled her to his chest and wept.

From under the bed, Eliana sobbed softly.

66

Emergency Physician Hospital Room 612

"I still need to talk to Beth LeHan." Sheriff Roy hit the mute button on the TV remote and motioned Jude and Gwen into his room. "If she can help expose JD's human trafficking ring, I believe I can get her cleared of any charges for her involvement." He adjusted his hospital bed to the sitting position. "And I need to see your brother Eric, too. Seems his prints turned up at a double-homicide in the Industrial Park."

"You can't believe he had anything to do with that," Gwen said.

"No, of course he wasn't there. The whole thing stinks of JD. I just need your brother to confirm a couple things."

"Maybe you should take it easy a couple days, Sheriff." Jude stood next to Gwen at the foot of his bed. "I mean, you've got a busted hip and you've been shot in the head."

"He didn't shoot me in the head," the sheriff corrected. "I just bumped it when JD pushed me." The sheriff allowed himself a quick smile. "That idiot tried to kill me with my own revolver. But there wasn't any bullets in those cartridges. Just a little gun powder. And my hip was old anyway. Pushing me down that embankment just forced me to get a new one sooner than I planned."

"Well, you've still had a rough week," Jude said.

"We all have," the sheriff glanced at Gwen. "Listen, I'm sorry about your aunt. Whatever her involvement was, she didn't deserve to be gunned down like that."

Gwen bowed her head. "Thank you."

"He'll pay for what he's done. I promise you both that. JD can't hide forever," Sheriff Roy's neck flushed. "He'll be brought to justice, one way or the other."

"There are still things that don't make sense." Gwen's head was still lowered. "I don't understand why he waited. If JD followed us to Beth's house, he knew Eliana was there, too. Why didn't he grab her then? It's like he was waiting for something."

"Unless it wasn't him," Jude said. "Maybe it wasn't JD who followed us to Beth's house. There are still two members of the High Echelon unaccounted for."

"I don't know, Jude. Just doesn't add up. Why would he even bother taking me to that cave?" Her eyes were distant. "What did he have to gain by leaving me there?"

"He doesn't have a plan." The sheriff growled. "He's just crazy. Crazy people do crazy things."

"I hope your right, Sheriff," she said. "I just hope he's not smarter than you give him credit for."

67

E ric sat on the floor with his back against the wall. His living room was dark.

Dark and cold.

His eyes traced the trail of dried blood that staggered across the carpet, leading to the hole where his front window had been. Shredded curtains rippled in the night breeze. Another winter storm was stirring in the west. Seemed to be a lot of storms these days.

It was midnight, and he had been here for hours. Watching and thinking. He needed to get away for a while, needed some time to wrap his head around the chain of events that had led him here.

Beyond the curtains was darkness, a numbing black interrupted only by occasional flickers of lightning and grumbles of thunder. If he could, he would blend into the night; just disappear and be gone forever.

There was still blood on his hands.

Her blood.

He couldn't bring himself to wash it off. He slowly rubbed his sticky fingers together and remembered her red hair. Remembered her smile. A gust rattled through his broken living room, but the chill didn't bother him; he really didn't feel anything right now. Or maybe he felt too much. He was aware the stitches on his arm were burning, but didn't care. Maybe this was how it felt to go crazy.

Indifferent.

Disjointed.

Numb.

Lightning stabbed the darkness again.

Her last words drifted through his mind like a ghost.

Watch Eliana.

That was all she said. She had given her life for his, and for what? For the life of a child? It made no sense. None of it made sense.

He rubbed his hands together. Her blood flaked and peppered the carpet around his feet as his eyes wandered to the leg of the coffee table in front of him. A piece of paper had been left for him; impaled on a shard of glass in the front window.

The note was now folded perfectly on the floor next to him. He had read it once, hours ago, and the words were etched in his mind. Playing over and over.

I told you I would kill you. How does it feel to be dead?

68

Katrina sat on her park bench and watched the oak's gnarled limbs stir the overcast sky. Today, the crows were gone. And honestly, she wasn't sure they had ever really been there at all. She tucked the pink strand of hair behind her ear and straightened her jacket. Her heart fluttered; she was nervous and wanted a cigarette. "No," she whispered. "I don't need those anymore."

The day on Swine Lake had been a turning point. Her nurse, Mag, had done something that no one had done since her father died.

She believed in her.

And she gave her a small, red New Testament Bible. The words were so tiny she got a headache the first time she tried to read them. But she did read them. And somewhere between Luke and Ephesians, Katrina found peace.

Two silhouettes rounded the gate. Katrina recognized the silver-haired woman who had taken her baby. The same woman who promised to find someone to love her baby was now bringing her back.

Sweet irony.

Tears rimmed her eyes as she stood and numbly walked toward them. They met under the arms of the oak.

"Katrina," Beth was unsure how to begin. "I had to find you. What I did to you was so wrong."

Katrina blinked away a tear and knelt in front of the child. Her little girl was beautiful. Tucked behind Beth's leg, she watched Katrina with curious eyes. Golden hair billowed from under her stocking cap. Katrina recognized her jade eyes from pictures of her own childhood.

"What's her name?" Katrina whispered.

"Eliana." Beth knelt next to Katrina and guided the child closer. "Her name is Eliana."

"Eliana," Katrina savored each syllable of her name. "I'm your momma."

"My momma?" She looked to Beth for approval.

Beth smiled and nodded, unable to speak.

"My name is Katrina."

Eliana touched the pink strand. "That's pretty," she said in her small voice.

"Thank you," Katrina said. "I did it a long time ago to remember you. I've been thinking about you every day, wondering if you were okay."

"I'm okay." Eliana shrugged her shoulders.

"I know. I'm so happy you're okay."

Beth knelt next to them. "Katrina, what I did was wrong." She slid off her glasses and folded them in her lap. "I lied to you. I told you I would keep your child safe; find a loving home for her. When I promised those things, I had no intention of keeping them."

Katrina brushed corn silk hair from Eliana's eyes. "We were both in different places then. I was wrong, too. I should never have abandoned her. I allowed my own shame and fear to decide my child's fate." Katrina gently rubbed her forearm. "But actually, you did keep your promise. You cared for her and protected her. You found her a loving home. Even though your intentions were evil, they were destined for good."

Eliana stepped a little closer to Katrina. "Are you coming with us to our new home? Because we're going to have a puppy." She was smiling.

Beth placed a hand on Eliana's shoulder. She didn't lift her eyes. "Eliana, you and your momma will find that new home and puppy—"

"Wait." Katrina blinked through stray tears. "A puppy? That's a wonderful idea, Eliana. I love puppies, too." She found Beth's eyes.

"You've been the only mother she's known. You've given her the childhood I was incapable of. And I can never repay that." She paused to consider her words. "But I do have one request."

"Anything."

"Stay with us and show me how to be the mother you've been."

Beth met Katrina's eyes. "After the horrible thing I did, you would ask me to stay in her life?"

"I'm asking you to stay in our lives. I need your help, Beth. I don't think I can do this without you."

Beth embraced Katrina. "I don't deserve your trust. But I would do anything for you and this child."

"It's settled then." Katrina gave her attention to her little girl. "And I have something for you, Eliana." She pulled the little Bible from her coat pocket. "This is a very special gift; it will always help you find what your heart is looking for. It helped me find you."

Eliana's little hands fit the Bible perfectly. She scooped it up with wide eyes and smiled.

"I don't think we should stay in Willow," Beth said quietly. "I know it's hard to just pick up and move like this, but it's still dangerous..."

"No, I agree. We can't stay here," Katrina said. "There's too many memories. Too much death. A new life deserves a change of scenery, I think." Katrina rose and traced the etched oak with her fingers. "I need to say goodbye to my grandmother. I want her to meet Eliana. I've been living a lie for so long, I don't know if she'll understand or accept any of this. But I won't hide the truth from her anymore." Her fingers lingered a moment over the three crosses. "And I want to say goodbye to Mag. She didn't even know me. I didn't think love like that existed. Not for me anyway." Katrina smiled at Beth.

"Then, we can leave." She paused to consider the decision. "Yes, I'm ready to leave this place forever."

They left the old oak to guard the etched memory on its bark. Three silhouettes walked through the gate as the day dwindled and dusk settled to blot out the remains.

Katrina glanced back at her tree. A whisper of sadness echoed through her soul as she remembered her family. She would always miss them, but she couldn't allow regret to smother her life any longer. It was time for her to live again.

Eliana's small hand reached up and gripped her finger as they walked, tugging Katrina's attention back to her new reality. Her new beginning. Her new family.

Even though the swirling voices were gone, Katrina expected the road ahead would be tough. She didn't believe in fairy tale endings, and knew the hope that ignited today was still vulnerable to darkness tomorrow. Just as trials follow blessings, shadows follow light. She watched Eliana shuffle along beside her, and smiled. *As long as we're together, I don't care about the shadows.*

Behind them, a February gust slammed the metal gate shut. Scattered leaves chased and spun in frigid circles. Quiet voices stirred through the limbs of her oak, swirling and dipping between its grey branches. Whispering voices that rose and fell like dark wings on the wind. The voices twisted down the base of the tree, settling at the feet of a man with dark eyes.

He hesitated a moment, considering the etched memorial on the tree before following the path toward the gate. Toward Katrina and her bright future.

It was true; shadows follow light.

They always do.

Epilogue

The Cellar Doors

The Ballistic Armored Transport rolled through the tall fescue, plowing tire tracks into the cold earth. Its diesel engine rattled obstinately, grinding to a stop near the base of the hill. A collection of emergency vehicles and a news van were already scattered around the perimeter of the field. Red and blue lights spun like an orchestra of fireflies in the dawn light.

"I want this area secured, gentlemen." Squad Commander Scevas slammed the passenger's side door and ripped his vest tabs, revealing a yellow SWAT patch. "Back those emergency vehicles another fifty yards out," he pointed at the fire engine and two civil defense pickups. "And send the press another hundred yards beyond that." He studied the twin wooden doors shadowed by the depression of the hill. "Michaels, get a light on those doors."

Within minutes, the eight-man squad was clad in body armor and black camouflage. They assembled in a loose band around Scevas.

"We go in with shotguns and NVG's," Scevas said to the circle of men as he pulled his night vision goggles over his cap. "We don't know what kind of terrain's in there, so take a set of rappelling clips and cables."

A stocky Korean named Lao spoke up. "What about taking C-8?"

"No. It'll be hard enough to see without a cloud of pepper gas to deal with." Scevas lowered his tone. "I spoke with the sheriff a few minutes ago. He's in the hospital with a busted hip, so he won't be here. But he thinks there's kids in this cave, which means our primary goal is rescue." He looked at each man. "Don't discharge your firearm unless you are absolutely positive of your mark. I don't want unsecured fire ricocheting around my head. And I certainly don't want to answer for a dead kid on the evening news." Scevas waited for heads to nod in agreement. "Okay, check your night-lights and mind your perimeters. We all go home tonight."

The squad gathered in front of the cave's throat. "Eight in, eight out," Scevas said. "Stay in constant sight of your partner. I don't know what tons of rock will do to our radio communication. If you're separated from the group, initiate your personal SGPS. The sonar component should guide you back to mobile command. If the SGPS gets glitchy, use your strobe beacon and don't move; I'll find you." Scevas pumped a shell into the chamber of his shotgun. "This is a cave, gentlemen; watch the shadows."

Fifty meters in, the shaft began a slow arc to the left. "Okay, gentlemen," Scevas' voice crackled in the team's earpieces, "we're about to lose the use of the B.A.T.'s spotlight. Once we round the corner, switch your night-lights to infrared and activate your goggles."

Michaels followed the path until he was out of the spotlight's reach. He snugged the optic lenses over his eyes and clicked his shoulder light to infrared mode. Through his goggles, the cavern blinked to life with an amber glow. He and Lao waited for the team to gather behind them.

"Base Alpha," Scevas whispered into his mic. "Disengage the spotlight. We're going dark."

Moments later, the halogen sun waned, leaving the cave black. "Gentlemen, from here on, we tiptoe. Keep it quiet and let's find those kids." Scevas lowered his voice. "Move out, Michaels."

Michaels shifted the strap holding his Remington shotgun as the cavern floor began to meander downward. An underground stream seeped from the walls, etching crooked fingers of water down the center of the walkway. It kept the ground slippery. A blanket of sludge sucked at the team's boots, slowing their progress and hindering their clandestine intentions.

Lao nodded to Michaels. "On the ground, to the right."

Michaels grunted an acknowledgement. "Got it," he said, crouching next to the object. "It's a metal stake. Like what they use on railroad tracks." He wiped a muddy glove on his pant leg and slipped a Zip-lock from his vest.

Scevas paused to scan the ground they had covered. The night-vision goggles used an infrared pulse from his shoulder light, which was amplified and translated to the optic lenses. The result was a crisp, red-orange illumination through the goggles, but near invisibility for the wearer. The tactical advantage allowed the squad to see in the dark without being seen. An advantage the bad guys didn't have. Scevas turned his attention to his team. Ahead, Michaels and Lao were at point, stooped over something. He tapped his throat mic. "What is it?"

"Metal stake on the ground. Looks like blood on it..." Lao's voice tangled with the radio static.

"Stow it and go, gentlemen; we're not here for souvenirs."

The team snaked through the cavern, blending into the inky blackness as the shaft continued its subtle descent. After a few meters, Michaels stopped short, raising a hand to signal. To the right, a wooden door pulsated with an amber aura through his goggles. Scevas slid to the front, orchestrating his team with sharp hand motions. Lao and Michael crept forward to engage. Sergeant Pat Moss led two men to the far side of the door as Scevas staggered the remaining men against the cave walls as cover.

Lao positioned himself against the frame of the door and held up one finger.

Two fingers.

Three.

Michaels slipped into the room, searching its corners through the sights of his shotgun. A table leaned against the far wall. Around it, broken candles littered the floor like scattered bones. The air was stale and old. On the back wall, a second door hung from twisted hinges. Sergeant Moss dropped next to Michaels and motioned his two men to take cover near the table.

Stepping over the broken door, Michaels swept the smaller room. Wet walls were riddled with deep crevices and the ceiling disappeared beyond his infrared light. "Clear." He tapped his throat mic. "Two rooms, both empty." His report was followed by static.

"10-4. Regroup and let's move on." Scevas' voice was barely audible over the fuzz.

Lao relaxed his grip on the shotgun. "It's definitely a cell," he nodded at the broken door. "If there's one, there could be others."

Michaels was staring at the table and candles. "Let's just find those kids and get out of here."

The team regrouped in the main shaft. Scevas, obviously disgusted with the radio static, jerked his earpiece out and motioned the squad into a tight huddle. Less than twenty meters ahead, the shaft split. The left side ran a few meters before dropping out of sight; the right pulled into a gradual downward spiral.

He whispered to Sergeant Moss. "Two teams. Take Michaels, Lao and Purg. Scout the right side."

Scevas took the remaining three men and spelunking equipment and edged to the left. He tapped his watch and signaled for both teams to rendezvous in thirty minutes. Then, sliding a canister from a vest pocket, he sprayed an arrow pointing toward the cave's entrance on the wall. The arrow glowed fluorescent in the amber light of the goggles. He glanced at Moss for acknowledgement of the orders. The Sergeant motioned for his team to follow.

The cavern floor became more narrow as the team spiraled. Moss took the lead, crouching behind his shotgun. Lao hugged the wall a step behind him, sweeping the darkness with an infrared spotlight. Michaels followed the new guy. He wasn't even sure what his real name was. They called him Purg; short for Purgatory City. He had transferred from Colorado two weeks earlier. For some reason, his hometown city stuck as a nick name. This was his first mission with the team.

Michaels remembered his own first day; a meth house bust in the East Side Boro. After pulling the bars and front door off the hinges, he was the second member in. He recalled two things: the smell of the house—a mixture of cat urine and body odor. And the dolls. There weren't supposed to be children in the house.

He found the little girl cowering in a bedroom closet. No more than five or six years old, she was squeezed in the corner with a dirty face and soiled tee-shirt. He would never forget the horror in her eyes. She was frightened of him. To her, he was the monster; not her crack-peddling mother.

He remembered scooping up the child and trying to comfort her. Trying to convince her it was all right; she would be safe now. But it didn't work. The more he tried to calm her, the more she screamed and pushed against him; crying for her stoned mother.

He knew removing her from that environment was the only chance she would have at a normal life. And maybe, if enough time passed, the psychological damage would be minimal.

One day, she might even thank him for ripping her from the only life she had known. But until that day, her screams still haunted his memories.

Michaels shifted the shotgun strap on his shoulder. The cave was growing warmer, which seemed odd. He assumed the farther down they went, the cooler it would get. A step ahead, Purg was breathing hard. *Nerves*. Michaels could relate; there was something different about this assignment. An underlying feeling of dread flickering at the edges of his mind.

Michaels remembered the nameless girl in the meth house; maybe it felt weird because this raid involved children, too.

He touched his earpiece. Nothing but soft static. Too far underground for radio communication, he decided. For assurance, he reached to the back of his utility belt and checked the snap on his personal SGPS device. Without radio communication, this was the only option for getting out of here.

At point, Sergeant Moss stopped short and dropped to a knee. Purg eased against the wall, shifting his shotgun slowly to his shoulder. Michaels strained to sort out the amber images. The cavern walls continued their slow descending arch to the right and the ceiling again faded to black; its height still lost in shadows. The walls were riddled with pockets and streaks of quartz, which seemed to move and shimmer in the electronic light.

Nothing appeared to be out of the ordinary, and he was about to question the sergeant when he heard the gentle sobbing.

A child.

Michaels popped out his useless earpiece and held his breath. The sobbing continued to rise and fall, echoing off the walls. They moved ahead slowly and deliberately, like cats stalking prey. Lao concentrated on the infrared spotlight, scanning for fluctuations in temperature; hoping to find the child in the darkness.

The crying became louder, growing in desperation. The cavern changed directions, snaking to the left before leveling out. The floor widened into an expansive room. Groups of pointed stalagmites twisted and rose from the floor to meet slivers of hanging stalactites. In the goggles' amber light, the crooked points shimmered around the perimeter of the room like broken fangs.

The sobbing filled the cavern, coming from the left. Or right. Or above. Michaels followed the sound around the room, trying to pinpoint its origin. He followed a vein of quartz up a nearby wall. It pulsated like a glowing lightning bolt up the curved ceiling. He searched the darkness above. The crying couldn't be coming from up there.

"Sergeant, to the right, three o'clock!" Lao was excited.

A small girl stood beside a column of stalagmites thirty meters ahead. Her mouth sagged open in a mournful wail. Moss held up two fingers and pointed at the girl. Lao and Purg moved forward. Michaels knelt next to Moss and clicked the safety off his shotgun. His stomach churned like a nest full of snakes. Uneasiness squirmed up his spine. The girl was young, maybe four or five with light-colored hair. Her lanky silhouette pulsated with an amber aurora in his goggles. She was wearing a man's tee-shirt which hung in tatters around her ankles. The snakes coursed through his guts. She looked familiar, a frightened face from his past. The snakes coiled, causing his stomach to drop.

Impossible.

The girl from the drug raid; the little girl who plagued his dreams. But she was safe now.

She had been given a fresh start at life. Adopted by a young couple from Nebraska. That was two years ago. Two years ago!

Michaels leaned against the cavern wall to catch his breath. He wanted to shout a warning but couldn't find his voice. His stomach was on fire; the snakes were constricting his lungs.

Something stirred above Lao's head, churning from the blanket of darkness above. Purg stopped and motioned for the sergeant. He seemed confused. And he was talking, something about the infrared spotlight. It wasn't working right.

He didn't see the shape twisting above him and Lao.

Michaels reached for the sergeant's shoulder, trying to get his attention. Every movement was in slow motion. He could only watch the drama unfold in front of him. Lao made it to the little girl first, kneeling next to her and speaking softly. The child closed her mouth and turned her head to face Lao.

"Get out of there!" Michaels found his voice and screamed at Lao.

The child grinned at Lao then vanished. She was just gone.

Michaels stumbled past Moss, trying to run. Trying to reach his teammates, but his legs were so heavy. They dragged like cement pillars and his stomach teetered on the edge of nausea.

The shadow swooped from the ceiling and consumed Lao. His terrified screams filled the room as he fought and swung at the darkness. He called for the sergeant, but his plea was cut off by a heavy thud and a short gurgle. The wet sound of meat being ripped resounded off the walls.

Purg dropped to the ground and rolled away. Sergeant Moss gained his composure and sprinted past Michaels toward Lao's body. A shotgun blast erupted from the corner of the room causing Michaels' goggles to flash white. He dropped to his knees, blinded by the glare. Ahead, he could hear Moss barking orders. Someone responded with a second shotgun blast.

Another scream.

Michaels stood and staggered blindly toward the commotion. The amber vision slowly faded back. Moss was swinging the barrel of his shotgun at the air above the fallen body of Lao.

"Sergeant!" Michaels closed the distance to his friend.

Moss left the ground, jerked up by an unseen force. Suspended in the air, he swung and cursed at the invisible hands.

"Pat!" Michaels' voice shook with fear and confusion.

A sharp snap of bones. The sergeant was thrown like a rag doll against the far wall; he dropped in the midst of the pointed stalagmites. Michaels sprinted after his comrade, dodging and weaving between the twisted shards. He found him lying on his back; a leg was twisted under his body. One of the smaller stalagmites jutted from his stomach. He was still alive but an amber pool was slowly tracing the outline of his body.

Michaels turned his attention back to the center of the room. It was quiet now. Sergeant Moss would die soon if he wasn't lifted off the spike. Michaels bit his lip; he shouldn't give his location away, but... "Purg! I need help. Come, quick!" He posted his shotgun against a nearby column of rock and held his breath, waiting for his echo to fade. Moss groaned, regaining consciousness. "Hang on, Pat; I'll get you out of here." A flicker of movement to the left caught his attention as he swung his shotgun and brushed the trigger.

Purg crawled out of the darkness; his goggles were missing. "Michaels? I can't see. Talk me in."

Moss groaned and tried to sit up. "Easy, Pat, try not to move." Michaels eased the sergeant back to the floor. A swell of blood bubbled around the protruding shard.

Purg felt his way to Michaels' side. "Did you see Lao? Did you see what happened to him?" Purg was on the brink of panic.

Michaels focused on the sergeant; his face was cool and his breathing had slowed to a heavy rattle in his chest. "We're losing Pat," he said, sliding the goggles from the sergeant's head and passing them to Purg. "Put these on; we've got to stop the blood."

"We've got to get out of here," Purg said, adjusting the goggles and taking in his surroundings. He shuffled backward, realizing he was crawling through a pool of the sergeant's blood.

"Help me lift him off this shaft," Michaels said, hooking his arms under the sergeant's armpits.

Purg scooped up Moss' knees and looked at Michaels. "He doesn't look good."

"On the count of three," Michaels said. Sergeant Moss wheezed and jerked as his body was lifted off the stalagmite. Blood splashed on the limestone floor, draining from the puncture. Somewhere near the center of the room, the gentle sobbing started again. Michaels' blood turned to ice. The sergeant's eyes rolled back as his breathing stopped.

"CPR, we've got to start CPR." Michaels swallowed the fear and snapped his attention back to his friend.

Purg was staring over his shoulder. "The boy is back." His words were barely audible.

Michaels began compressions on Pat's chest. The rhythmic sloshing drowned out the hollow whimpering stirring around the room. He panted over the body, stopping to check for a sign of life. "We need to get him out of here."

Purg was still preoccupied. "That boy," Purg began, "I know that boy."

Michaels paused to listen for a heartbeat. He wiped a bloody hand across his forehead.

"He's my cousin's son," Purg continued.

Michaels searched for the sergeant's vitals. It was obvious he was gone; too much blood loss.

"Michaels, did you hear me? That's my cousin's son." Purg was unraveling. His voice shook as he whispered.

"Purg, I didn't see a boy; I saw a little girl."

"And the infrared gun—" Purg continued, "it didn't pick up his body heat. It registered everyone else: you, Lao, Sergeant Moss. But not him." His voice trailed as he focused on the sobbing. "Michaels, my cousin's son is dead."

Michaels stood and reached for Purg's shoulder. "We're backing out of here, Purg. Rejoin the squad and get help."

Purg turned to face Michaels. "Did you see what happened to Lao?"

"No, let's go."

"He was torn apart. I was right there."

"We're leaving, Purg." Michaels knelt next to the still body of Pat and unsnapped the Glock from his shoulder holster. The words of Commander Scevas rang in his mind, *We all go home tonight...*

"I'll come back for you, Pat." He promised his dead friend. "I'll take you home."

TO BE CONTINUED IN BOOK TWO

SHADOWS OF WILLOW

Enter the Cellar:

Password: Akeldama

Cellar Doors

Read on for an excerpt from

Shadows of Willow

by
Lance LaCoax

The sequel to

CELLAR DOORS

A Novel

Shadows of Willow

The storm fell in brutal sheets across the two-lane highway; roaring against the windshield. Dane jerked the steering wheel to straddle the wet tire indentions tracing the curvy road. The bald tires would hydroplane given the chance, so he hugged the right shoulder and gripped the wheel in the ten and two o'clock positions. He hated driving in the rain, especially at night.

Thunder clapped above the treetops as he clicked the high beams and shifted into fourth. His CD player blasted a *FlyLeaf* track, but he barely noticed. Lightning splintered the sky, outlining the highway in jagged white. Dane squinted at the flash and slammed the brake pedal with both feet. His Honda slid sideways across the double yellow line, toppling a green mile marker before stalling to a stop.

He leaned against the steering wheel and cursed under his breath. "Who in their right mind...!?" He focused on the rear view mirror. On the road's edge, a white-washed cross stood outlined in bicycle reflectors; a silent reminder of an automobile tragedy. The reflectors winked at him between waves of rain.

But the cross marker was not what caused him to run off the road. He rolled his window down to clear foggy glass and search the highway's shoulders. Rain spat at his face, blurring his vision. "Couldn't have been. No way someone's out here in this." He pushed the clutch and turned the motor.

Another flicker of lightning traced the silhouette of a face watching him from the passenger's side window. Dane's foot slipped off the pedal, causing the car to lurch forward and sputter to a halt. The door snapped opened to a thin-faced man with dark eyes. He slid into the seat uninvited and slammed the door.

"My, it's wet out there," the man shook rain from his collar.

Dane caught his breath, not sure if he was more shocked by the audacity or nonchalance of the guy. He wasn't sure what to say.

"What are you doing?" was the best he could do.

"Oh, looking for a ride," the man ran fingers through his wet hair. "Lucky you stopped for me."

Dane regained his composure, "Well, actually, I didn't."

"Didn't what?" The man shook rain from his hair and offered Dane a crooked smile.

"I don't pick up hitchhikers," Dane was gaining his confidence. "I mean, I don't usually."

"Don't usually?" The man asked, "Then I guess your hypocrisy is my salvation."

"Where are you going, anyway?" Dane ignored the rebuke. "And where's your car?"

"She's in a ditch; out of gas," the man said. "And it doesn't really matter where I'm going. The real question is, where are you going?"

"Home. I mean north," Dane sounded unsure.

"So, I suppose that's where I'm going, too." The man was still smiling. "You can drop me off at the first gas station on your way home. I mean north."

Dane stared at the steering wheel a moment. "Yeah, okay. I can do that." He glanced at the man; "You're not like, an axe murderer or anything, right?" Dane tried to disarm his apprehension with humor. He forced a smile.

"Now where would I hide an axe?"

Dane's smile faded.

"Right."

He leaned on the clutch and cranked the ignition. *Flyleaf* blared to life:

'...*I'm so sick*
infected with
where I live
let me live
without this
empty bliss
selfishness...'

Dane checked the rearview mirror and slid into first.

"Why did you say, '*she's* in a ditch'?" He asked.

The man was staring at the radio.

"Sorry." Dane turned the volume down a little. "Your car, you said *she* was in a ditch. How do you know your car is female?" The quiver in his voice betrayed his attempt at humor. "I mean, how do you tell?"

"I'm curious," the man responded. "Are you a man of faith?"

Dane hesitated. "What's that got to do with the gender of your car?"

"You know, go to church, read a Bible. Things like that."

He paused before answering. "Sure. I go to church sometimes."

"So, you believe in angels."

"You mean, like guardian angels?"

The man flashed his teeth. "Precisely. Do you believe you have a guardian angel?"

Dane shifted uncomfortably in his seat. "Sure, I guess so. I suppose it's possible we have angels around to protect us from bad stuff." Dane glanced at the man. "Why would you ask me that?"

"Then you must believe you have a demon that follows you around, too."

"What?"

"You certainly can't believe in one without the other." The man wasn't smiling; it was more of a sneer.

Dane focused on the road; it was raining harder now. "I don't know about that." He couldn't think of anything funny to say.

"You don't know about that?" The man repeated. "If you believe in angels, you can't deny the logic of demons. A guardian angel needs something to protect you from. Every shepherd needs a wolf to make the sheep feel safe."

"I don't know, I guess." Dane slid as close to his door as possible.

The man's dark eyes drifted to Dane's throat. "So, do you think he ever takes a break, or maybe gets preoccupied?" The man was still sneering. "Do you think your little guardian angel ever wanders off?" He leaned closer to Dane, "What would your demon do then?"

Dane couldn't look at the man. He reached for the volume knob on the CD player. His hand was shaking.

The man reached into the shadows of his trench coat as lightning curled and twisted around the angry sky. Streaks above the passing tree line illuminated the interior of the car for an instant. Thunder vibrated the highway.

The Honda coasted to a stop in the middle of the road.

"And to answer your question, I wasn't referring to the car as a *she*. And *she* certainly didn't ask as many questions as you."

Dane's head slumped against his chest; a dark blotch spread around the hilt of a hunting knife lodged in his chest. A gurgle of air leaked from a punctured lung.

The man turned his attention to the blaring music. "Emo music creeps me out a little." He jabbed the eject button and tossed the disk out the window. "Let's find something a little more soothing. Something to settle the nerves." He twisted the radio knob, finding the public radio station. "Ah, a night with the classics." Bach's haunted strings crackled through cheap speakers.

"This is definitely more like it, don't you think?" He glanced at Dane's crumpled form. "What's that?" He listened to words that were never spoken. "Oh, of course. How inconsiderate of me. You would be much more comfortable in the backseat."

Special Thanks...

D an and Candy, the sounding boards and adult voices of reason to my childish imagination (Candy, how many times did I make you read this thing?). My friends at Buffalo River Coffee Company for a seat in the corner, an exceptional house blend, and occasional forensic help. Sissy (you're next), Jess, and Shelby for the late-night edits and honest opinions. Nathan, Chris, and Wikipedia; my esteemed panel of professionals. Ryan and Shawn, it was like Christmas every time you guys sent an email.

And of course, my Jen, who believed my silly story could help shed light into the dark corners of someone's life.

I have been, and always will be your greatest admirer.

And Sarah— no, you can't read it yet.

About the Author...

When asked to write something interesting about myself for this section, I couldn't help but smile. I mean, who really cares about an unknown writer? From a literary point of view, I'm quite the bore. This being my first published work, there's nothing to compare it to. And to be honest, my life outside of writing is pretty boring, too. Never travelled anywhere significant, never met anyone famous, don't have any cool scars.

So, I decided instead to paint the backdrop of *Cellar Doors*. A sort of verbal portrait of the scenery and circumstances which led to the conception of the story.

The idea began in the fall of 2002, around the time the Beltway Sniper was terrorizing the East Coast. My family and I were living in Virginia Beach, and I recall the apprehension I felt each time our car's gas gauge leaned toward empty. Dreading the idea of being a potential target, I would coast into a station on fumes, pump as much as my nerves would allow, and speed away like my life depended on it.

One particular night, I was on my way to Sandbridge Beach listening to the latest report of the shootings. There were conflicting statements of what the sniper was driving, if he was hunting alone, and where he may strike next. At the time, it seemed law enforcement knew very little. I think it was that horrific unknown that scared people the most. I know it scared me.

It was getting late and, as usual, my tank was on empty. The last chance for gas was a Shell station ahead and around the bend. As I approached, I remember noticing the brightly lit SHELL sign positioned just above the station. A second glance dropped my heart to my feet as I realized the 'S' was burned out, leaving an ominous crimson HELL suspended in the dusk sky.

I took it as a sign (pun intended) and didn't stop for gas.

Instead, I sped home and scribbled the experience in the form of a short story. I drafted a couple pages about a poor soul named Ted who finds himself at a HELL station and ends up fighting for his life.

A few days later, the sniper was apprehended and life fell into its hectically normal cycle. My story lay forgotten in a drawer next to my bed for a few years until my dad let me borrow a book by Bill Weise. *23 Minutes in Hell* documents the author's supernatural experience which lead him to believe Hell was literally in the center of the earth. Mr. Weise's vision intrigued me, and also reminded me of my forgotten scribbled story. The pieces began to connect and a tale was born.

Now, for those who know me, writing a book like *Cellar Doors* may seem a little out of character. I'm not exactly the most serious guy in the room. Humor has generally been my social crutch. But, as the story began to take shape, I found common ground with the characters. The struggles and fears they each faced were familiar. I saw the faces of Kat, Eric and Jude reflected in many lives around me. Real life is not always pretty. Not always bright. Sometimes, a soul lost in the dark craves more than just humor. Sometimes a flashlight is more practical.

My hope is *Cellar Doors* will be that flashlight to someone wandering in the dark...

Lance LaCoax lives in Middle Tennessee with his wife Jennifer, their four children, and two spoiled cats. When not quoting movie lines from Star Wars or Napoleon Dynamite, Lance pretends to be a superhero.

Jen actually is one.

Please visit

www.**cellardoorsbook**.com